LEGACY OF
"THE CAUSE"

AN ALTERNATIVE HISTORY NOVEL
OF THE AMERICAN CIVIL WAR

MARK B. FOOR

PublishAmerica
Baltimore

First printing

This is a work of fiction. Names, characters, places, and incidents either are the product of the author's imagination or are used fictitiously. Any resemblance to actual persons, living or dead, events, or locales is entirely coincidental.

PublishAmerica has allowed this work to remain exactly as the author intended, verbatim, without editorial input.

ISBN: 1-60703-368-2
PUBLISHED BY PUBLISHAMERICA, LLLP
www.publishamerica.com
Baltimore

Printed in the United States of America

DEDICATION

In memory of my father, Maynard J. Foor, who left me the legacy of a great love of learning. And also to my mother Sallie Garee who has always believed that I could be and do anything I wanted. And also to my reenacting family both here and passed, I love each and every one of you more than you will ever know!

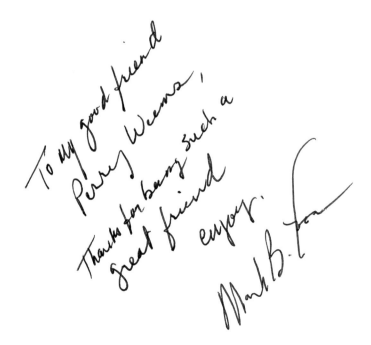

"War is a continuation of politics by other means."

—Carl Von Clausewitz

"Rich man's war, Poor man's fight."

—Common Saying of Civil War Soldiers

A WORD OF THANKS

It is my opinion that a work of this magnitude is not created solely by a single individual but is built upon the work of other writers of the genre. It is with that thought in mind that I wish to express my gratitude to the great writers and chroniclers of Civil War history. Their names are as well known as our own but none has influenced me more in this endeavor more than the late Shelby Foote. It was his commentary on the PBS documentary by Ken Burns that really brought the Civil War to life for so many of us. His written works carry the same trademark hominess. His influence will be greatly missed. Now at last he has an opportunity to get the facts straight from the men that fought that Great War. I can almost picture him sitting under the trees on a crate, discussing strategy with the likes of Grant, Lee, Hancock, and of course, Jackson. This work would be impossible without their monumental contributions. Equally important in this process are the many people who have helped me and at times put up with me in the pursuit of this dream. I want to dedicate this book to them. First, I want to thank God for allowing me to exist in this time and place. To my mother, who taught me the value of determination. To my Father, God rest his soul, who taught me a love of learning new things. To my wife, Mary and my children Brianne and Ian, thank you for being there and supporting me through all of the ups and downs of the creative process. And finally to all my fellow reenactors, the men, women and children who take so much time and effort to research their particular impressions and then give of their time, money, blood (usually fake, although sometimes real), sweat (remember, we ARE talking 100% wool!) and tears (anyone who has ever pitched a tent at night, in the rain will understand), you folks are the greatest! It has been an honor to know each and every one of you. See you at the next event!

FOREWORD

As any writer will tell you, a book begins with an idea. This book is no exception. Several years ago, I got the idea that I might like to try my hand at writing a work of historical fiction. However, life is what happens while you are making other plans. After several job changes, a couple of kids and other assorted tragedies and joys, along with much encouragement from family and friends, what you see before you is the result of that idea.

As a long time student of American history in general and the Civil War in particular, I have always had the same thought as many others. What could have been and what would have happened if the South had gained its independence from the United States? This book explores one possible alternate reality. The major difference between other books of this type and this book is that this story does not involve things such as time-travel, magic or other such flights of fancy.

As a Civil War reenactor, I have devoted a great deal of time to the study of the mid-nineteenth century and of the War itself. I have tried to provide a balanced, plausible alternative to what history has written without taking sides in the politics of the day. I have merely taken what was and raised the question "what if this had happened instead of this?" Hopefully I have accomplished what I set out to do in giving the reader something to contemplate about this defining moment in American history.

PROLOGUE

After two years of bloody fighting and terrible losses on both sides, the Army of Northern Virginia and the Army of the Potomac now stand poised for a battle of gigantic proportions not only in terms of combat effectives involved but also in terms of the importance of the outcome.

In command of the Union forces is General George G. Meade a capable, if not always enthusiastic commander. His 95,000 men have been shadowing the movements of Robert E. Lee's Army of Northern Virginia up the Shenandoah Valley through Maryland and into Pennsylvania. Lee's plan is to drive into Pennsylvania, placing his army between the Union forces and Washington, D.C., forcing President Lincoln and the United States government to sue for peace.

Outnumbered, Lee's 75,000 men have attempted to screen their movement by keeping behind the Blue Ridge Mountains. Conventional military wisdom of the day dictates that the cavalry leads the army and acts as it's eyes and ears in enemy territory. Under the command of General J.E.B. Stuart, the Confederate cavalry seemingly fails in this mission by leaving Lee's army to stumble blindly about until a chance meeting of skirmishers takes place in a small Pennsylvania town with little or no military value except for the fact that it will unwittingly become the focal point of the war's most critical battle to date.

CHAPTER 1
FORTUNES OF WAR
GETTYSBURG, PENNSYLVANIA
JULY 1, 1863

The day was hot, dry with no promise of rain in the clear, blue sky. This fact was not lost on the soldiers of Brigadier General John Buford's cavalry division as they watched from the cupola of the Lutheran Seminary building the slowly approaching mass of gray and butternut clad men who were stirring up the dust of the road with their mostly bare feet.

Earlier in the day, local militiamen had skirmished with an advance party of the Army of Northern Virginia that had been out foraging, hoping to find a supply of footwear that was rumored to exist in the town. After being pursued through the town, the militia had linked up with Buford's men who fought as dismounted cavalry and managed to drive off what was later determined to be elements of Heth's Division of A. P. Hill's Corps.

Buford understood the importance of the ground on which his men stood and the heights to his rear. He knew that the infantry support that he desperately needed was several hours away under the command of one of the army's best officers, John Reynolds. Sensing that there was an opportunity and an advantage to be gained, Buford positioned his men across a broad front along and below the crest of Seminary Ridge with their orders to hold the enemy in place and "stack them up". He knew that the longer he held this line, the more time he would buy for Reynolds to bring up his infantry support and the longer it would take the Army of Northern Virginia to sort itself out and deploy in anything that closely resembled an effective line of battle.

This singular act was one of many that made it possible for the Army of the Potomac to gain the advantages that it possessed at the end of the first day's fighting. Precious little was gained by the Confederates at day's end and General Lee knew that he must find a weak point in the Union defenses if he had any hopes of carrying out the bold plan first devised between him and President Jefferson Davis several months earlier in the latter's Richmond residence.

One thing continued to occupy Lee's mind as couriers from commanders all over the field brought reports and requests for instructions and re-supply to the farmhouse that now served as the Headquarters of the army.

He wondered, "Will it work, can they get here in time and unobserved?"

Colonel Taylor was just ushering in another courier, taking from the man a small scrap of paper, a brief message to the Commanding General from a subordinate who was eager to report any and all possible advantages to be gained whether real or imagined. Lee smiled inwardly as he thought to himself, "When did I become this symbol? I have never aspired to such a lofty position."

For a moment he reflected on his narrow escapes and his failures of the past 2 years. He had been fortunate that the Federals had not had better leadership. An abler commander would have been able to seize opportunity and done a great deal of damage to this army and in turn to the fledgling country that it represented.

Reports from all up and down the lines of the two armies seemed to reflect similar thinking on both sides. After the intense fighting of the first day, the positions of the two armies had stabilized and it looked as though neither one was in any hurry to leave their opponent in command of the field. As Lee made his final troop dispositions for the night and prepared to get as much sleep as he could on the eve of another days fighting, he said a silent prayer that nothing would interfere with what could be the one gamble that would bring this awful conflict to a successful conclusion.

JULY 2ND

Colonel Joshua L. Chamberlain's 20th Maine Regiment had been marching all night when they arrived at the foot of the Round Tops early on the morning of July 2nd. As part of the 5th Corps they had moved up from Virginia through Maryland by way of South Mountain and were nearly exhausted when they received their orders from Colonel Strong Vincent. They were to take a position at the extreme left of the Federal line and were tasked with the protection of the flank of the entire Federal army. After taking heavy casualties at Fredericksburg and then the debacle of Howard's Corps at Chancellorsville, the 20th Maine was at less than half strength and not even the assignment of 120 men from the old 2nd Maine could engender much hope in the officers and men as to their success in the coming fight if they met with anything more than a token show of force which their position in the line would almost assure would never happen. Chamberlain knew the importance of their situation and he was determined to hold this piece of ground at all costs.

The Confederates came at first light starting at the extreme right of the line situated on Big Round Top and came under heavy fire from regiments from New York and Pennsylvania. Several batteries of artillery were hauled up the side of the hill and entrenched to support the regiments defending Big Round Top. Losses were heavy including Colonel Vincent and several other ranking officers. Despite the losses, the lines held and the Confederates continued to move to the left, probing the lines for weaknesses to exploit. By the time they reached the ground in front of the position held by the 20th Maine troops, it was the 15th Alabama Regiment under the command of Colonel William C. Oates that was tasked with rolling up the Federal line just as General Rodes had done at Chancellorsville.

Chamberlain and his men fought like men possessed and only after depleting the majority of their ammunition did Chamberlain order an unlikely military maneuver gleaned from a French manual on military tactics from the time of Napoleon. The maneuver was sufficiently obscure that the Confederates never knew what was coming and when it did, they fled before the bayonets of the Maine men like wild game before a forest fire. It was only after the remaining Confederates had fled down the hill and the gruesome task of rounding up prisoners and caring for the dead and wounded began that Chamberlain heard the sound of battle coming from a direction that he knew that there should be none.

Hurrying back up the hill to the summit of Little Round Top, Chamberlain scanned the countryside with his field glasses and to his dismay, he realized too late that the attack that he and his men had just fended off at such a high price was simply a diversion to draw attention away from the real focal point of the attack. Looking at an area to his rear that showed signs of a great battle, Chamberlain thought to himself, "They've gotten between us and Washington, what shall we do now?" Little did he know the extent to which they had been deceived.

The reports came in to Meade's Headquarters slowly at first but then more and more rapidly as the cavalry patrols and the units involved in the day's action reported the sights and sounds of battle in areas where there were previously reported no enemy movement. From all of the bits and pieces of information three things became increasingly clear.

First, John Bell Hood had not attacked through the Devil's Den as the Federal high command had anticipated. Instead he had swung his division far around the right in a long looping maneuver, using the attack on Little Round top and a small demonstration to his front to mask his movements and then swung back around on the back side of Little Round top to disrupt the supply of men and supplies to the units positioned there and on Big Round Top.

Second, McLaws' division had taken the Peach Orchard and the Wheatfield and held on stubbornly for several hours depriving the Federals of reserve troops to devote to the shifting of the battle lines. Had these troops been available, it is possible that the threat to the Union rear would have been able to be negated.

The third surprise that Robert E. Lee had for George Meade was the sudden and unexpected arrival of the man that everyone had been led to believe was dead. Even a large majority of the Army of Northern Virginia had mourned the loss of their beloved "Stonewall" Jackson, who now brought a fresh corps of his "foot cavalry" up through Winchester, Virginia where he linked up with General J.E.B. Stuart who had just arrived from Rockville, Maryland and George Pickett who brought his division from Gettysburg via Cashtown. Jackson sent Stuart ahead as his cavalry vanguard to lead a surprise raid into western Maryland and positioning himself squarely between Washington City and the entire Federal army. The panic that set in served the Confederate purpose even better than they had hoped.

At the White House, President Lincoln had been meeting with his cabinet to discuss the current operations taking place in Gettysburg when he received dispatches and telegrams warning him of the approaching Confederate force. He immediately dispatched a squadron of cavalry from one of the units whose task it was to protect Washington from just such an attack if one ever came. His orders were simple, find the enemy, determine to the best of your ability their intentions and exploit any weakness that you may find to your advantage.

After several hours of probing and sharp skirmishes in the surrounding countryside, a courier was sent back to the White House with information for the President. He learned from the man that the force that was attacking Washington was comprised entirely of hardened combat veterans commanded by two of the most capable officers that the Confederate Army possessed. When a telegram was received later that afternoon from the commander of the cavalry detachment requesting instructions as to whether or not to admit an officer of the Confederate force into Washington under a flag of truce and with a full military escort, Lincoln knew that he was being rapidly backed into a corner and that he had to make a decision fast and it had better be the right one.

The information that President Lincoln had received from Gettysburg had indicated that there had already been a great loss of life on both sides and that further fighting would only add to that number. He had, for months been getting pressure from the War Democrats or Copperheads as they were known, to seek peace with the Confederacy if the opportunity presented itself. It was now becoming clear that that moment was at hand. Lincoln wired his cavalry commander to escort the officer directly to the White House and that he would be interviewed to determine what his and his government's intentions were.

Lincoln expected to be speaking to a field grade officer, some low level functionary of the Confederate high command. He was, however, shocked and surprised to learn that the officer delivering the pre-planned correspondence from Jefferson Davis proposing peace talks was none other than Jackson himself.

The tall lanky Confederate General was ushered into the Oval Office by an army Major who saluted first his

Commander-in-Chief and then the visiting officer, as military protocol demanded when facing an officer of higher rank. Jackson first rendered a crisp military salute to Lincoln acknowledging the former's office and then turning to the Major with a wry smile on his face gave another perfect salute and said, "Thank you Major, you have been most kind and a perfect gentleman."

The Major returned the salute and said simply, "Thank you sir, I was only doing my duty." With that, the Major turned and left the two men alone in the Oval office where Lincoln offered Jackson a seat and said, "Well now General, let us see what your President Davis has to say about this somewhat awkward situation that we find ourselves in".

Jackson silently appreciated the predicament that the President of the United States was now facing. Should he fight on or should he seek peace and let the Confederate States go their own way? Lincoln knew that the Confederacy had for many months now been getting support from England, tacitly at first but now it was becoming more and more overt.

The U.S. Navy was having an increasingly difficult time intercepting the ships that the British were sending carrying all sorts of civilian and military goods to the embattled Southerners. Their method was simple yet effective. They would send a large, ocean-going vessel to the outer limits of the United States' territorial waters bordering the disputed southern states. From there the ships would be met at night, usually under a full or nearly full moon by smaller, faster blockade runners who would then transfer cargo and set sail for whatever open port that they could reach either undetected or without getting themselves blown out of the water.

From there, military supplies were offloaded and transported to government warehouses and safe distribution points where they could be dispersed to the Confederate forces that most needed them. As for the civilian supplies, these would be taken into any number of besieged cities and sold at exorbitant prices to people who were being slowly starved and battered into submission.

Lincoln read and reread the brief letter penned by his Confederate counterpart in Richmond and was surprised at the lack of demands, which one would be expecting in a letter dictating terms of surrender. It seemed to Lincoln that Davis was not indeed demanding surrender but the opportunity to meet with Lincoln to discuss the manner in which the Confederate States of America would be allowed to become the sovereign country which she had been professing she was over the last two years.

Lincoln sent for a scribe to draft a proposal for a Peace Conference as suggested in Davis' letter. Lincoln suggested Baltimore as the location for the meeting since it was technically in a neutral state and the distance would be only slightly more advantageous for Lincoln than Davis. Passes were prepared to allow President Davis to pass through Union lines unmolested in order to attend the conference. He would be allowed a cavalry escort of no more than ten men and would be allowed to bring only one of those along to Baltimore to act as his Aide-de-Camp. Lincoln would observe similar guidelines himself and he already had the man in mind to accompany him. It was to be none other than his own son Robert. Lincoln thought, "Robert will see this and he will learn that at the end of war, whatever it's outcome, you must have peace and it must be a just peace."

In Richmond, Jefferson Davis was going through the dispatches on his desk, which were coming in from all fronts. In Gettysburg, Lee's Army of Northern Virginia had achieved complete surprise against the Army of the Potomac and George Meade. The two armies had fought to nearly a stalemate when the other part of Lee and Davis' plan had been discovered. Fortunately for Lee, Davis and the Army of Northern Virginia, the plan had not been uncovered prematurely as had Lee's General order # 9. That had had the potential for disaster written all over it had it not been for Lee's adversary at the time. Had George McClellan acted upon the information contained in those orders, he could have destroyed the Army of Northern Virginia in total; the war would have been over scarcely before it had begun.

Davis breathed a silent prayer of thanks that it had not been so. He also prayed for the souls of all of the men lost in this war and especially in the past two days. He thought to himself, "Perhaps they will be the last; perhaps we can conclude this business without further bloodshed."

At that moment, Davis' wife Varina came into his office and he could tell that the rumors had already begun. She rushed into his office and, as he rose to greet her, she threw herself into his arms weeping with joy at the prospect of an end to the country's troubles. She said, "Oh my darling, now perhaps all of those people who have been blaming the troubles of our country on you will see that you have had all of our best interests at heart all along!"

Davis gently kissed his wife's forehead and said, "Yes my dear, perhaps, but we mustn't get too confident about these sudden successes. There is still much work to be done and it may take many years to re-build what we have lost and to get our country back to being the place that we all remember. And I fear that I will not have a say in what is done for much longer. You must remember that my term of office is only for another three years and I cannot be reelected as President Lincoln can. Still, I will do what I can for the length of time that I have remaining in my term. First, I shall have to meet with President Lincoln to discuss what terms shall apply to the cessation of hostilities, and then I shall have to see what is to be done about securing what we will need to re-build our country. Perhaps we shall send ambassadors to England and to France to see if we might be able to establish friendly commerce with those countries."

Davis made a mental note to himself to talk these ideas over with his cabinet. "They should be able to put something together to establish our bona fides" he thought. After a time, Varina gained some of her self control back and left him with a kiss on the cheek saying, " Perhaps we should plan some sort of a state dinner to begin establishing diplomatic ties with our neighbors to the North as well as courting a few European nations for the sake of commerce." At this, Davis stared at his wife in shock. He had never known her to be interested in politics in the slightest. Just when he thought that he knew this woman, she surprised him with her wit and her precise understanding of most any political situation.

The representatives of the two warring nations met on September 3rd in Baltimore, Maryland at the home of that state's governor. Lincoln, accompanied by his oldest son Robert, a captain in the U.S. Army, arrived first and was greeted by the governor who made a great show of treating the Lincolns to every first class accommodation at his disposal. He effusively thanked the Chief Executive for giving him the opportunity to serve in this elevated capacity. Lincoln assured the man that the idea to meet in Baltimore was as much Davis' idea as it was his. Just when Lincoln thought the man was about to fall prostrate and begin licking his boots, a butler appeared in the doorway of the Governor's office and announced the arrival of President Davis and his single escort, a young, handsome, bearded cavalry officer resplendent in a fine gray uniform with large amounts of gold braid and the collar insignia designating him as a General officer in the Confederate army. The Governor did not have to be told who the officer was, the fine uniform, the boyish good looks and the easy smile combined with the cavalier boots and the hat festooned with a large black ostrich plume meant that this could be none other than General J.E.B. Stuart.

CHAPTER 2

NEGOTIATIONS

BALTIMORE, MD

AUGUST 15, 1863

The four men faced each other across the large, ornately carved oak table that normally served as a meeting place for the top-ranking political figures of the state of Maryland. A tray of fruit, cheese, and sweetbreads sat virtually untouched at one end along with bottles of wine and other spirits as well as pitchers of water and a tray of fine crystal glasses. At the moment, there was a heated discussion as to the future of several areas of what was soon to become the "former" United States of America. The word was quickly spreading that the war could be over in as little as two weeks and that the U.S. government was preparing to pull all of it's troops and ships out of those areas that were now being claimed by the newly liberated Confederate States of America.

"Sir, I am simply saying that I cannot unilaterally give you the New Mexico territory without first consulting with the Supreme Court and Congress," Lincoln stated in his soft, but firm way as a father might scold a favorite child.

Davis sadly shook his head and said "Mr. President, I am sure that you would agree that by conceding the New Mexico territory to the Confederacy, you will be creating a buffer between the United States and that ambitious French maniac Maxmillian!"

"Agreed" said Lincoln "But as much as I might want a wall between the United States and Mexico, I have to try and do what I think is in the best interest of the people living in that area. What are you going to do with the land there? God knows you can't farm it and most people don't want to intentionally move there."

Davis smiled at this and said something that took Lincoln by surprise. " We are going to allow the Indians to set up their own state that will be largely run by the native peoples but we in the Confederate government will have a say in many of the larger issues that the creation of this nation-state will cause, he said."

Lincoln nodded and said simply, "That's a pretty good plan to keep them happy. At least then you won't have to worry about chasing them all around the desert like we've been doing the last 10 years. I will put your proposal to the Cabinet and Congress and the Supreme Court. I will telegraph you as soon as I have their decision. Now there is another subject that I would like to discuss with you since we are trying to work out a deal. What shall we do about exchange of prisoners of war? We can't very well just turn them loose can we? Doing that would almost certainly cause problems wherever they went due to the already depressed condition of most of the homes and farms both North and South."

Davis thought about this for a moment and then said, "What we could do is to have the men go to the nearest large city or town and once there their names could be recorded and then arrangements be made for them to be transported to the nearest population center and from there they could arrange to either be met by a friend or family member or they could have the option to hire transport to their homes."

Lincoln nodded and said, "It just might work. We would have to make arrangements to transport the sick and injured to places where they could receive proper medical treatment for their individual conditions."

Davis nodded at this and said somewhat ashamedly, "Especially those poor devils at Andersonville. I want you to believe me when I tell you that I had no idea what that maniac Wirtz was doing there. Had I known, I would have gone there and removed him from command myself."

Lincoln smiled sadly at his counterpart and said, "I understand completely Mr. Davis, and I have had a similar problem with the people running Elmyra. I hear that it is nearly as bad." Davis nodded as if to acknowledge that he had heard the same things about the Union prison for Confederate prisoners in New York State.

After 2 weeks of intense negotiations, the two Chief Executives finally agreed and drew up an agreement that ended the bloodiest conflict on the North American continent and shaped both the nations and the destinies of countless millions of people for many years to come. Both men secretly prayed that they could continue to hold their respective countries together until cooler heads could prevail on a number of hotly contested issues that had yet to be decided.

Just when it seemed that the new Confederate States of America were off to a flying start and the United States was slowly getting back to normal, two separate events seemingly unrelated but more than coincidental occurred which threatened to destroy both nations in detail. Little could anyone imagine the far-reaching shock waves that would shatter any illusions that anyone on either side had of a quiet return to the peaceful days that they knew before the war started. It all started on a quiet evening in Washington while the President and the Mrs. Lincoln were attending a performance of a comedic play at the city's pre-eminent venue for the performing arts, Ford's Theater.

CHAPTER 3

CLOSE CALLS AND CONSPIRACIES
FORD'S THEATER, WASHINGTON CITY

The President and Mrs. Lincoln were seated in their box on the balcony level of Ford's Theater and after the obligatory applause and the waving and shaking of hands, the audience was settling in for the opening act of the play. Just a few blocks down the street in a dimly lit saloon a lone figure stood at the bar drinking a glass of brandy, a fact that had not escaped the notice of several of the bar's regular patrons. The handsome, mustachioed, smartly dressed man was a virtual unknown to his fellow drinkers. Had this been a New York or London establishment, the wealthier, better-educated clientele would have instantly recognized the man as the world famous stage actor, John Wilkes Booth. Booth chose this establishment for just that reason. He was in Washington, not as an actor on the stage but an actor in a play that would either end in triumph or tragedy for his beloved South.

Booth left the saloon and rode the 2 blocks to the theater and entered through the performer's entrance. Having been there many times he wasn't even challenged by anyone in the theater's side room. He paid a boy $2.00 to go outside and feed and water his horse and told the boy to have the horse ready to go when he came out. Having secured his mount, he turned and headed into the main part of the theater. He felt the weight of the small pistol he carried in his coat pocket and thought about the papers he carried in the breast pocket of his shirt. His orders were quite clear. His assassination of the President would be the signal for a series of actions that would ensure the future of the Confederacy. The thought of that gave him a sense of calm that told him that no matter what happened to him, the way of life he had come to love would be safe if only the others could carry out their parts of the plan.

Booth walked through the lobby and garnered nothing more than a casual glance and a nod from one of the ushers as he headed for the stairs leading up to the Presidential Box. When he reached the top of the stairs, he reached for the doorknob and, slowly turning it, he started to make his way into the box when he was confronted by a Union Major who was persistent in his inquiry as to Booth's identity and the reason for his presence in the President's private box. With almost imperceptible movement and reflexes like a rattlesnake, Booth shouldered his way past the officer while at the same time slashing at him with a large knife that he had pulled from his waistband. The officer cried out as Booth rushed past him and, as he rounded the corner and saw the familiar form of the President before him, Booth pulled the small pistol from his pocket and aimed at the back of the President's head.

Just as he pulled the trigger to fire the shot that would truly set his country free, Booth felt something like a large snake wrap itself around his legs and he felt himself losing his balance. Before he could improve his stance and take the shot, he pitched backwards and reflexively pulled the trigger, sending his single bullet into the ceiling above him. His head struck the floor hard enough to send a kaleidoscope of colors cascading through his brain and just before he lost consciousness, he saw the bloodstained blue uniform and then the face of Major Rathbone whom he had just tried to kill. With a sort of detached sense of curiosity, Booth wondered how the others had faired. He hoped that despite his failure, the plan to free his country from the yoke of the oppressor would still succeed. He had no idea yet how complete his failure would be and what the consequences of that failure would be.

Booth slowly felt himself coming awake and almost immediately he was aware that his hands and feet were bound to the chair on which he was sitting. He had the strange sensation of being underground and that there had not been any fresh air in the room for many years. There was very little light but still Booth struggled to see where he was. After a few moments he realized the futility of the exercise and started to focus on what was going to happen next and why he had been spared.

From one side of the room, which was hidden deep in

shadow, a deep, booming voice spoke. Even though the voice spoke barely above a whisper, Booth felt the reverberation of the rich, bass notes off of the stone walls and they seemed to penetrate through him and he was instantly filled with the sensation that this was the voice of Death itself. "Who ordered you to kill the President?" the voice asked.

Booth considered his options and decided to try and play it cool. "My dear fellow," he said, "I have no idea what you are talking about. My actions were entirely my own."

At this there was an almost imperceptible movement from the direction of the voice. At the conclusion of the movement, Booth heard movement behind him and almost instantly, his body was wracked with indescribable agony especially in the area around his shoulders. It was now apparent to Booth that he had been mistaken about being tied to the chair. Only his ankles were tied to the chair itself. Now, it seemed that his arms were simply pulled behind him and a rope was fastened around his wrists. The movement behind him that he had been unable to witness was when two men simultaneously hauled up on the rope, which had been threaded through an iron ring that was secured to one of the roof beams. The resulting sudden rotation of his shoulders in a direction that was not only foreign to the joint but also very stressful to the other structures in his upper body such as ribs, collarbone, sternum and shoulder blades caused a degree of pain that, had he been asked on a previous occasion,

Booth would have never thought possible for the human body to endure.

After remaining suspended like this for what, to Booth seemed like an eternity but was in actuality a few minutes, the rope was suddenly slacked and, although there was relief, there was also the pain of bones and joints suddenly, and in some cases violently returning to their original positions. Only a great deal of self control kept Booth from crying out in agony. He lay on the floor suddenly relishing the coolness of the stone and the brief comfort it gave his tortured body. His revelry in his newfound comfort was short lived. Presently, two pair of hands roughly seized him; paying no heed to the pain he had just endured and placed him back on the chair. Once again, his arms were bound behind him but not to the chair.

The voice spoke once more. "Mr. Booth, we have your weapons and all of the papers that you carried on you at the time of your capture. We know that the person who gave the orders is acting outside the sanction of the Confederate government. All we want to know is who is it and what are they trying to accomplish?

This time Booth tried the silent treatment, saying nothing and hoping that this would be interpreted as an unwillingness to aid an enemy. Several moments passed and just when Booth thought he had won and there would be no more punishment, a man stepped into the dim lantern light from the direction of the voice. Booth realized at once that he would never be able to identify his tormentor since a crudely made hood obscured the man's face. All that was visible to Booth were the man's eyes and when Booth looked into their icy blue depths, he was instantly terrified at what he saw, or didn't see because when he looked into those eyes he realized that he was looking at a man without a conscience and most probably, without a soul.

The man's movements were quick and there was little or no wasted motion. He simply reached down to Booth's feet and with a small knife, cut the ropes that secured his ankles to the chair. Interpreting this as a gesture that he was about to be freed, Booth said, "I appreciate the fact of what you are trying to do but by now you must be aware that no matter what you do to me, you will never get me to say anything incriminating."

At that Booth began to stand up as if to give his captors clear access to the ropes binding his wrists behind him and just before he reached his full height, the man in the hood nodded and Booth's arms were suddenly wrenched behind him and he was hauled up until only the toes of his boots touched the floor.

"Alright, Alright I'll tell you what you want to know," whimpered Booth.

He had endured what by now seemed like days of this repeated lifting and pulling until he was quite sure that both of his shoulders were broken. His hands and fingers had become numb almost from the beginning. As he said it he felt instantly ashamed that he had been captured and broken. He chided himself for not being tougher and that despite all of the boasting and thoughts of bravado, he was a weak man after all.

Pinkerton, nodded to the man in the hood from the doorway where, unseen by Booth he had orchestrated the whole interrogation. Pinkerton knew that many of his methods were on the fringe of being illegal themselves but he rationalized that the fate of the nation hinged on his ability to get adequate information to prevent any more such episodes as the one that had been carried out the night before. Pinkerton was a patient man so he allowed Booth to regain consciousness unaided and then had the interrogation conducted in such a way as to maximize the effect of the techniques and their ability to gain information and at the same time minimize the lasting effects. Pinkerton wanted Booth to be in perfect health when the Supreme Court sentenced him to hang in this very room in the basement of the old Washington Navy Yard.

The President was resting comfortably in his room on the third floor of the White House. He was sitting in bed wearing his spectacles reading through some papers that had been brought up to him by his personal secretary, John Hay. Hay had taken to being the President's self-appointed guardian after the assassination attempt. At first it was a simple matter, keeping the knowledge of the President's injuries from the public. But someone put out the word to the press that contrary to the government's position that the President had not been injured, He was taken from Ford's theater under heavy guard and that a physician had been summoned.

The physician examined the President and pronounced that he was not in any immediate danger. The bullet had hit the ornate brass chandelier and ricocheted back and struck the President in the chest just to the left of the sternum and below the rib cage. Because the bullet had expended most of its energy striking the chandelier, it did not have sufficient energy to enter very deeply into the body. It was a small matter for the doctor to anesthetize the President and in a few moments he removed the bullet, cauterized the wound and sutured the skin. No internal organs were damaged worse than a slight bruising. The doctor ordered ice packs for the surface bruising and bed rest to allow the body time to repair itself. He left specific instructions that the President not over exert himself, an instruction that the President's secretary took as a personal mission.

Lincoln was busying himself reading documents. He made notes on some and added his signature to others. He looked up when there was a knock on the door. "Come in.," he said. The door opened a crack and Hay's head and right shoulder appeared. "Sir, Mr. Pinkerton to see you. Are you well enough to have a visitor?"

Lincoln laughed at the young man who had appointed himself as Lincoln's personal nursemaid. "Yes, Yes, Mr.

Hay, I feel fine, just a little sore is all. Send Mr. Pinkerton in, I am sure that he has something of great interest to say."

"Yes sir" the young man replied. And with that the door opened a little further and Hay stepped aside to admit Alan Pinkerton into the President's room.

Alan Pinkerton wasn't a tall man he was however very powerfully built, owing to a life of hard work both in his native Scotland and in his adopted country. He entered the President's room and removed his hat, suddenly seeming humbled at being in the presence of the President in his bedroom and realizing just how close he came to losing his boss.

"How do you feel sir?" Pinkerton asked.

Lincoln smiled at the almost child-like reverence that he now saw on his Secret Service chief's face. "I am fine Mr. Pinkerton. I assume that you have news for me of some importance?"

Pinkerton nodded and said, "We think that we have gotten all of the information that we can get from the prisoner. His story is that he was acting on the orders from the head of the Confederate intelligence agency and that he was only part of a much larger operation."

Lincoln thought about this for a moment and said, "How much larger Mr. Pinkerton? What other surprises do we have to worry about?"

Pinkerton stared at the floor a moment and said, "We're not sure sir, Booth only knew that there were other agents with other assignments. He didn't know who they were or what their orders were. Everything that they are doing seems to be highly compartmentalized. Maybe their troop movements from Gettysburg were another part of the plan. It could be that they felt with their troops menacing the city and you dead, the government would be more likely to treat with them on their terms."

Lincoln looked at his security chief and said, "I hope you are right. But why would they try to kill me after the Peace conference had already concluded?"

Pinkerton thought about that for a moment and said, "Either he didn't get word that his mission had been called off or maybe he wasn't thinking rationally and decided to try to kill you on his own accord. Either way, we have prevented him from carrying out his mission and now we will see how brave he is when he faces the hangman's noose."

At that, Lincoln spoke up and said, "He will need to be tried first and if the court decides against hanging, we must abide by that. In the meantime, we must be sure that we have every piece of information of value from him. We need to question him further about what is going on in the South, what is their economic situation and what are they doing to stabilize their government?"

Pinkerton suddenly stood upright with a look of disbelief on his face.

"What is it?" the Lincoln asked.

"Something you just said made me think of something

that Booth said during the interrogation. He said that several of their junior staff officers and some pretty high ranking field officers were recently arrested and that several of them had been tried and hanged. When asked why this had happened, he said that he didn't know the whole story but that it had something to do with the British observer, Fremantle, I think was the name Booth used."

Lincoln's eyebrows arched when he thought of the possibility of England taking a more active role in the war. "Thank goodness that never happened", he thought. Little did he realize that what he was witnessing was just the groundwork for a larger plan that would be years in the making.

At the same moment that Pinkerton was reporting to President Lincoln, in Richmond, a man stood before the desk of Jefferson Davis holding in his hand a small piece of onionskin paper and said to the President of the Confederate States of America, "Sir, the attempt on Lincoln failed. Our agent was captured and at this moment is probably being questioned by the U.S. authorities, possibly even the military. He strikes me as being a fairly strong individual and I do not expect that he would be grossly mistreated by the Yankees."

Little did the man know that at that moment, Booth was in his cell in the old Naval Prison not knowing whether more torture or possibly even death awaited him outside the door of his cell. All he did know was that he had been broken both physically and mentally. He could not remember everything that he had told the Yankees but he knew instinctively that it was more than he should have.

Booth lay on the bunk in his cell staring up at the ceiling and thought about the turn of events that had ended with his capture and imprisonment. He thought about the short time that he served in the Richmond Grays and how he had quickly realized that he did not possess the necessary backbone to lead the life of a soldier on the battlefield. It didn't take him long to figure out that because of his chosen profession, he was uniquely suited to one of the more dangerous and somehow strangely enticing roles of warfare, that of espionage.

Because of his seemingly innate ability to affect certain personae, he was the perfect choice to send on many of the missions for which he had selected. It had been a small matter to have the theater company Booth performed with scheduled to appear in many of the areas of the North that the Confederates needed intelligence on. Booth's keen mind and the memory that allowed him to memorize volumes of Shakespeare and Ovid and many other playwrights and poets, also allowed him to memorize details about the movements of the Northern Army that the newspapers seemed to consider to be nothing more than a device for them to use to sell newspapers.

It was no wonder that General William Tecumseh Sherman had made the statement, "We could kill every reporter in the country and there would be news from Hell before breakfast."

Booth thought about this and chuckled to himself at the irony of his plight. He stopped laughing after only a few seconds though, owing to the numerous fractured ribs that his hooded tormentors had given him. There were also numerous cuts and bruises not to mention the fact that both of his shoulders had been nearly ripped from their sockets.

Booth suddenly realized that at this point, only two choices and two fates awaited him. His choices were, escape and risk re-capture only to face the wrath of his superiors in Richmond. His other choice was equally dismal. Stay where he was and probably be tried and convicted of espionage and then await the sentence that he knew would come...Death. He didn't know how they would execute him.

He thought, "In war time, one would expect that the standard method would be firing squad." Although after some thought, Booth determined that no, since he was essentially a civilian acting in an unconventional manner, the most likely method that would be used was hanging. Booth thought of the prospect of meeting his end at the end of a rope and the idea did not appeal to him in the least.

It was because of this that Booth began to plot how he could escape this ghastly Yankee prison and take all the information that he had gathered prior to his arrest and 'interrogation' and somehow get it back to Richmond so that at least there might be a way to use the information to somehow gain the upper hand when dealing with those blasted blue devils.

CHAPTER 4

POETIC JUSTICE... OF A SORT
THE OLD NAVAL PRISON, WASHINGTON

Just as Booth was musing about his plight and how he might escape his captors to report his findings and the results of his mission to Major Norris, Davis' chief spy, he did not notice the shadowy figure of Allan Pinkerton watching him from the doorway of his cell.

"Not thinking of leaving us just yet are you Mr. Booth?" The actor/spy/would-be-assassin started at the sound of the deep, booming voice that suddenly echoed off the stone walls of the cell. Pinkerton stood watching the man's reaction and was inwardly pleased that he had managed to put the fear into him. "Well, no matter, the High Court has agreed to hear the case against you tomorrow morning and I wouldn't be at all surprised if they came back with a verdict in the same day.

Booth was suddenly very frightened. He had considered that there would be swift justice involved but to have the Supreme Court hear the case and so soon after the "crime" had been committed. Booth still had trouble considering what he had done a crime so he was not well prepared to face any type of punishment much less the severe type reserved for those who attempt to kill kings or other heads of state. Booth did his best to conceal his true feelings at that moment but he could not help but think of some of the plays that he had acted in that dealt with just this type of situation.

He could not help but think, "Shakespeare had the right idea when he wrote 'Julius Caesar' and 'Othello'. It never dawns on you until you have failed that you might actually face some sort of retribution in the end." At the thought of this, Booth's heart sank. He now realized that he would never leave this prison cell unless it was to go to his death.

As if he could sense what Booth was feeling and thinking, Pinkerton said almost mockingly, "Oh, don't worry, I'll make sure that they put the knot right so you don't suffer, which is more than you deserve you murderous bastard!"

Booth's head snapped around to face his tormentor just as he realized what Pinkerton had said. So, it was to be the gallows. Booth knew that what Pinkerton had said was all too true. If the knot of the noose were not placed just right, the prisoner would endure a slow, agonizing death from asphyxiation, rather than the quick and relatively painless end from a broken neck and severed spinal cord.

As if to punctuate the moment's finality, Booth could hear activity in the courtyard below, but since the windows of the cell were set high in the wall, he could only guess that the sounds were those of men building the scaffold that he would have to climb. Proof of this arrived just moments later when Booth could hear sawing and hammering below. He cast his eyes first to the window above with its heavy iron bars and then to the floor as if to signal his resignation to his fate.

Pinkerton now saw that the man was completely broken and that there was nothing further that could be gotten out of him no matter how much they might torture him. Pinkerton turned and left the prison and signaled the guard to lock the heavy oak door. He was on his way back to the White House to report to the President that everything was in readiness to execute the prisoner once the Court had passed sentence. As he walked toward Pennsylvania Avenue, he had no way of knowing that the man in the cell behind him had just come to understand what lay in store for him and had begun to experience a complete mental breakdown which would last the rest of that day and night and well into the next day, causing the postponement of the carrying out of the sentence passed down by the High Court.

After allowing Booth two full days to regain something of his composure after he had been informed of the Court's decision, which had only taken twelve minutes to decide, the Government decided that it was time to put the matter to rest and that this process would begin with Booth's execution. Booth's last hours were spent eating a last meal, reading some books of plays and poetry borrowed for the occasion from, of all places, the White House library. Booth seemed to have gone back to being his former self and was unusually calm for a man who had only hours to live.

At precisely 6:00 PM, Pinkerton, escorted by two armed soldiers, entered Booth's cell and placed him in shackles and manacles. His arms were bound behind him at the elbows, which, Pinkerton noticed, caused Booth a great deal of discomfort. After this was accomplished, Booth was led, hobbling out the door into the courtyard. After his eyes had adjusted to the light, Booth saw in front of him the instrument of his death. It was at this point that Booth's panicked condition returned to him. He began to struggle and his legs lost their will to stand.

At a signal from Pinkerton, a small platform of sorts was brought up by two other soldiers and, together with the two men in the escort guard, they managed to wrestle Booth onto the platform and secure him to it with leather straps passed through slots cut into the wood. When he was subdued enough that they could ease their grip on him, the four men took up the corners of the platform and bore it like a stretcher towards the gallows. It took nearly ten minutes for the men to ascend the thirteen stairs to the main platform bearing their load between them.

Once at the top, the straps were removed after Booth's legs were bound at the knees to prevent him from collapsing again. He was then moved to a spot on the forward edge of the platform that upon closer inspection was nothing more that a couple of foot-wide boards being held upright by posts at either end. After he was positioned and it was determined that he would not cause any more disturbances, Secretary of War Edwin M. Stanton read the charges, specifications and the sentence of the Court. After he completed the reading, Stanton nodded to someone in the small group of people seated to one side as observers on another part of the platform. Many of them carried parasols and umbrellas to shield them from the elements, which at this time of year were unpredictable at best.

It was because of this that Booth could not see whom Stanton had motioned to until at last a tall, familiar figure rose and approached the spot where Booth now stood. Lincoln walked gingerly over and stood scant inches away from the man who, just a couple of weeks before had tried to kill him.

He looked at Booth for a few moments and then said, "Mr. Booth, I cannot pretend to understand what motivated you to commit the heinous act for which you have been convicted and now requires of you your life. I can however tell you that whatever gains you or the people you worked for had hoped to make, it has all been for naught. We will find those people like you who wish to continue the War and to further advance the gains, which your 'country' has already made. We will find them and we will try them and convict them and we will punish them to the fullest extent of the law allowed. But before sentence is carried out upon you, I feel that it is both my duty as President of the United States as an example to the people of this country and my duty as a Christian to tell you now that I bear you no malice for what you have done. You did what your conscience led you to do and now I must do what my conscience leads me to do. Having said this, may God have mercy on your soul." With those words, Lincoln turned to the officer in charge of the platform and said simply, "Carry out your duty, Major."

As soon as Lincoln stepped away from the prisoner and uttered those words, the officer turned and nodded to a lieutenant standing behind Booth. The lieutenant placed a hood over Booth's head and as soon as the hood was in place, the hangman placed the noose over Booth's head and positioned the knot behind his left ear. The hangman nodded to the Major and he in turn looked down to the ground at a sergeant who was waiting for a pre-arranged signal. The officer removed his hat and dropped the hand holding it down to his leg. This was the signal that the sergeant was waiting for. He turned and nodded to the men positioned under the platform, beside the posts. When he nodded the four men, each holding a large wooden mallet with a long handle, swung them and knocked the posts out from under the four ends of the board.

As the posts were driven out from under the boards, the boards themselves fell to the ground from under Booth's feet. In turn, since he no longer had anything to stand on,

Booth's body fell some six feet until it reached the end of the rope and his downward momentum was stopped, suddenly. True to his word, Pinkerton had indeed made sure that the knot was positioned properly and when Booth's body reached the end of the rope's limit, his neck was suddenly and violently broken by the combination of velocity and resistance. His death was indeed sudden and almost totally painless.

As the crowd started moving away from the scene, Booth's body was taken down and moved to a small room inside the prison where it would be prepared for transport back to his family so that they could observe whatever burial rites they chose. A statement released by the White House to the press later that week said simply, "The matter is concluded, justice has been served, and we wish to know his name no longer." Thus ended, for most people, the whole sordid affair. Little did they know that there were other matters that would soon make their presence known which would quickly overshadow recent events.

A few days later in Richmond, a man sat in an office reading a newspaper report on the death of a prominent stage actor who had been tried and convicted on a charge of attempted murder of a sitting President. The newspaper article was very detailed in its description of the scenes from the execution. William Norris, head of the Confederate Intelligence Bureau, closed his eyes for a moment and said softly, "Damn".

He had been counting on Booth's success on his

mission to pave the way for the other operations that were in motion at this very moment. He thought about all of the time and effort put forth on behalf of the Crown and the rewards for his service that had been promised by Queen Victoria, carefully routed through Palmerston and Fremantle and others.

He had personally spent months carefully hand picking the dozen or so officers, which he had cautiously approached and through a variety of methods ranging from payoffs to favors, promises of advancement and blackmail, had arranged for them to side with him in a quiet overthrow of the Davis administration. Now that plan was in jeopardy and he had to quickly assess to what extent his operations had been compromised. He unlocked his desk and from one of the drawers withdrew an odd-looking brass disc made up of two concentric rings.

On the outside ring were the letters of the alphabet. On the inner ring was a series of letters, numbers and weird symbols. By turning to the letter in either a clockwise or counterclockwise direction, the user was presented with a number, letter or symbol, which represented the actual letter in the original message. He simply needed to make an indication as to which direction that the wheel needed to be turned. He did this by indicating a for a clockwise turn and a for a counter clockwise turn. Each letter of the word then became a 2 symbol block.

First he sat with a pad of paper and drafted a short

message that would be transmitted in code to the conspirators in the coup. He then took up the disc and a pencil and, going letter by letter, he coded the message so that only his operators would be able to decode it. His last step was to walk over to the telegraph key that was a permanent fixture in his office and sit down and begin to tap out the coded message to each of the dozen or so men involved in the plot to overthrow Davis. He could not know that Booth had revealed most of the plan including many names of the participants and many of the proposed targets during the lengthy "interrogation" sessions in the Naval Prison's cell.

But Lincoln did know about the plan and he realized that a military coup at this point in the young Confederacy's life as a nation would likely destroy all that remained of the South's pride as well as its ability to remain a viable nation. It seemed to Lincoln that it was far more dangerous to have a nation on your Southern border in the throes of a military coup than simply having an armed nation that close. It was because of this that Lincoln sent a special dispatch rider with a message to President Davis warning him of the impending operation. To his credit, Davis actually set plans in motion to uncover the entire conspiracy and punish those responsible. After just few days all of the men involved were tried, quietly of course, and sentences were handed down which Davis himself personally signed.

The men who had been identified as the main

ringleaders of the coup attempt were all sentenced to hang. The rest of those involved received sentences commensurate with their level of involvement. Most of these would be imprisoned in the infamous Libby Prison in Richmond. The prison had been the scene of a daring escape by a number of Union officers that had been held there since their capture during the war. Their escape route had been discovered after the fact and, before the new inhabitants took residence, it was completely demolished or filled in to prevent its future use.

The lone exception to the punishments meted out was Norris himself. It was thought that if he were left unmolested, he would lead Davis and his investigators directly to the people that had orchestrated the entire chain of events. However, Norris proved to be a better spy than anyone imagined and when he became suspicious of the fates of his co-conspirators, who had suddenly become very difficult to contact, he simply changed his appearance and disappeared from sight. Some speculated that he had killed himself and still others came closer than they knew when they theorized that he had found passage on a ship leaving Virginia headed for Great Britain

CHAPTER 5

CHANGING OF THE GUARD
RICHMOND, APRIL 1867

It was a beautiful spring day unlike anything anyone had seen in many years, especially those years of the war. New growth trees tried their best to hide the deep scars that two and a half years of war had left on the countryside. There were wildflowers in bloom, birds singing and the people of the capitol city were out almost as if nothing had ever touched this part of the country. The air was full of a sort of excitement that was almost palpable.

Today was an historic occasion. Today the Confederate States of America would do something that would solidify them as a viable nation-state. They would hold their first Presidential election. Under the terms set forth by the Confederate States Constitution, the president was eligible for a single, six-year term. At the end of that term, he would step aside and another man would take his place. The purpose of this was to allow a sitting president the opportunity to accomplish as much for the people as possible but not enough of an opportunity to set himself up as a dictator.

Inwardly, Jefferson Davis was glad that his term was ending. He had seen his country through the darkest times and had helped it gain it's independence despite the many calls for his resignation during the war and the widespread distrust of his reconstruction policies of dealing with the United States as a trading partner. There were many who felt that normalizing relations with the United States was a tacit admission that the Southern Nation as some called it, could not survive without assistance from the parent nation. Despite all this, Davis had seen his country rebuilt and restored, at least partially, to its former greatness. It would now be up to his successor to further advance the task at hand.

Voting turnout had been high and there was no shortage of ambitious men who were seeking to succeed him. There had been fully twenty candidates from a variety of parties that appeared on the primary ballot. The early elections held to narrow the field had reduced that number to four with the law of the land being, regardless of party, the two candidates with the highest number of votes would serve as President and Vice President respectively. It was thought that if two men of differing political ideals were made to serve together in the two most powerful positions in the country, compromise would come almost as natural as breathing. The one factor that almost no one had counted on was the vote of the soldiers and former soldiers of the Confederate Army. It was they, through a write-in campaign that had caused the most profound event on the political landscape of the time. Despite his protestations that he did not desire the post, General Robert E. Lee, General-in-Chief of the Armies of the Confederate States of America was nominated for election to his nation's highest office.

Also appearing on the ballot was another former general officer and one that caused a great deal of commotion and argument among voters. James Longstreet was the choice of the fledgling Southern Republican Party to represent their interests in the election. Their premise was that the new Republic that they had fought so hard to found should emulate more closely the Republic that they had fought to separate themselves from. This did not sit well with the average Southern voter since the industrialization of the North was, in many opinions one of the main causes of the tensions between North and South leading up to the war.

Longstreet answered his critics by saying, "We need more of the types of businesses in the South that are currently in operation in the North. It is only through some degree of modernization and mechanization that we can hope to reduce our dependence on manufactured goods from the United States and elsewhere in the world."

The newly elected president and vice president would be faced with a problem that would threaten their country's very existence. At that very moment, several British ships of the line had taken up station along the coast of the Confederacy. It was the opinion of many of the political experts that the Crown was trying to intimidate and influence the incoming administration into being more receptive to British influences. Virtually every one of the candidates had published a statement decrying the action as "saber-rattling on a dangerous scale". The Davis administration had, without alerting the public and indeed many in the Confederate Congress, ordered the continuation of construction on a secret weapon that would change the face of warfare forever.

When it was begun in the fall of 1864, the program had been little more than an exercise on paper to see if the type of weapon that they had envisioned could be built with the manufacturing capabilities that existed at the time and if it could be built, could it be successfully deployed. The early studies had determined that such a weapon could be built and construction had been begun but budget and security concerns had caused the program to be placed on an indefinite hold. Now with the implied threat of invasion looming, Davis ordered that construction be resumed. Due to a severe shortage in funds, outside sources of financing were sought. Many affluent Southerners who had managed to preserve their resources were courted and one man answered the call out of an overwhelming sense of national pride. That man was Horace L. Hunley.

Construction of the C.S.S. Hunley, named for the generous benefactor who was paying for it, was a ship unlike anyone working in the Gosport Naval Yard had ever seen. She was a ship designed to operate *under* the water.

She was powered by hand instead of steam and she had but one weapon, a spar mounted torpedo, which could be affixed to the wooden hull of a ship by means of a large harpoon-like device and, through the employment of a long lanyard, detonated from a safe distance of up to one hundred feet or more.

Like all other inventions, the Hunley had her fair share of problems. Unfortunately due to the nature of the environment that she found herself in, her problems were most unforgiving. During one of the earliest trial dives to test her propulsion and surfacing and diving capabilities, she developed some sort of problem. It was either the detachable keel plates used as ballast to keep her submerged but which could be un-bolted to allow her to quickly surface or the sea cocks located inside on large, open vats that allowed seawater to be pumped in and out to create negative or positive buoyancy. Whatever the cause, the effect was disastrous. The Hunley sank to the bottom of the Chesapeake Bay, taking all hands, including H.L. Hunley himself to their deaths.

Undeterred by the loss of the crew, the Hunley was raised, her crew buried with full military honors and a new crew formed under the command of an Army lieutenant, George Dixon, who had survived the terrible fighting at Shiloh and had come back seemingly without fear of death in any of its many forms. Some speculated that this was due to the loss of his fiancée who had rushed to be at his side and nursed him back to health only to be killed herself when a ferry on which she rode was shelled by Union guns and sank.

Whatever the reason for his demeanor, Lt. Dixon was the perfect man for the job. He accepted nothing less than absolute loyalty and devotion to duty. He demanded perfection in the performance of that duty and, perhaps most importantly, he did not ask anything of his men that he himself was unwilling to do. This meant that if the situation demanded it, he himself would take a turn at the large cranking lever that provided the Hunley with both forward and reverse mobility. It also meant that, contrary to military practice of the time, Dixon ate, slept, drank and, sometimes brawled, right beside the men of his command. A fact which brought no great joy to the man who had been chosen, or condemned, depending on who you asked, to head up this program, General P.G.T. Beauregard.

It was Beauregard's design of the spar-mounted torpedo that had solved many of the Hunley's early navigation and maneuvering problems. Beauregard had little faith in the undersea boat, an opinion shared universally throughout the Confederate Navy and the source of more than one fight between the crews of the Hunley and any one of a dozen Confederate surface ships. It was widely held by Navy personnel that anyone who sailed in a ship that ran under water, out of the sight of the enemy was nothing more than a coward who chose not to defend his honor as a real man would. To the men who sailed the Hunley, this was the ultimate insult given the fact that they routinely faced dangers that these top water sailors would have no knowledge of.

Now in 1867, with the tensions between England and the Confederacy and rumors of an attempted British takeover of the new republic, the Hunley and her crew were called into service. Three years of refinements to the design and construction had left the Confederacy with a ship that was probably a hundred years ahead of its time. No longer did several men have to turn a large crankshaft that ran the length of the ship. Now a pair of hands could, through the employment of a reduction gear mounted in the stern of the ship turn the propeller just as fast and with greater ease and less fatigue than the old design.

Gone too were the keel plates. Now instead, enclosed tanks fore and aft had both seacocks and pumps to allow flooding the ballast tanks, as they were now called, with seawater to achieve negative buoyancy and then pump them out and replace the seawater with air to achieve positive buoyancy. This allowed the submarine to carry the same crew compliment as before and allow them to take turns at the various stations to prevent them from suffering from fatigue.

Another refinement, which increased the submarine's effectiveness, was the addition of a long tube protruding out of the dorsal surface of the ship. Called a snorkel, it allowed fresh air to be brought into the ship periodically when the ship was not in danger of being fired upon. The snorkel could be closed off by means of a sea cock and made water tight allowing the ship to submerge and make her attack or make good her escape after an attack. The viewing ports were redesigned to allow a better field of view and at the same time the turret, which held them, was adapted with plates at radical angles away from the triple pane glass to deflect any stray rifle shots or shell fragments that might otherwise endanger the ship and her crew.

All of these refinements and improvements were all well and good but in order for the cost in terms of time, money and lives to be worthwhile, the Confederacy needed to have a president that would be willing to use such a weapon if the need arose as well as men to sail her and command her. The outgoing administration was so impressed by the performance of this vessel Davis ordered 2 more ships just like it to be built. The Confederate Treasury Department sought out new sources of funding for the project and found that H.L.Hunley had willed the Confederate government several hundred thousand dollars to further their efforts to build a submarine force. It seems that he had foreseen the need for several of these vessels and had wanted to provide for their construction even in the event of his death.

With the funds secured and construction under way, the election of 1867 overshadowed everything else and Davis knew that he would have to brief his successor on the project as soon as the transfer of power was made. He silently hoped that the man chosen by the people would have the firmness of purpose to use these ships if they were ever needed. His prayers were answered better than he could have possibly hoped. When the votes were all submitted and tallied, Robert E. Lee won handily over the other candidates with Longstreet coming in second by a narrow margin.

Davis greeted Lee in the office of the President which he would soon be turning over to Lee. For his part, Lee had been gracious accepting the will of the people saying, "I have served the people of my home state of Virginia for all of my adult life. I will not turn my back on the people for whom I went to war. We have made a new country and God willing, we will keep it free. I shall endeavor to do my best as it would not be proper for me to do anything less."

Both Lee and Davis agreed that it seemed especially appropriate that the two men who would occupy the two highest positions in the country would have served together in the war. Indeed, many people thought that it was the will of God that the two men who were instrumental in creating the country should now be chosen to lead it. Lee and Longstreet were both surprised at the margin with which they won. Many people speculated that the reason for the high numbers was due to the former soldiers and current soldiers who still thought of the two men as their commanders.

Lee and Longstreet were sworn into office a week later on the steps of the Capitol building. The biggest surprise at that point had been their election, but that paled in comparison with one of the speakers that had been invited to the inauguration. President Lincoln had graciously accepted the invitation to speak at such an auspicious occasion. Lincoln himself was nearing the end of his term in office and had made it clear to the press that he would not seek a third term.

There was speculation that only part of the reason for Lincoln's decision was due to the injuries that he had sustained in the attempt on his life in 1865. He still showed signs of the lasting problems that the wound had caused him. Another reason that he chose not to run again, was due to the death of his son Willy. Willy had become sick late in the President's first term and the President mourned the loss of his child and felt the pain more deeply than most people could understand.

The only person who grieved the loss more than the President was Mary Lincoln. It was rumored among the White House staff that the First Lady was not mentally stable to begin with. She would launch into tirades and threaten those around her when she took to what the President referred to as "one of her spells". It was then especially hard when she witnessed her husband almost murdered before her eyes. Then to suffer the loss of a child in this manner, She finally suffered a mental breakdown that had prompted Lincoln's eldest son Robert to try and convince his father of the need to have her treated in an asylum where she could receive the care she needed.

After much begging and cajoling, Lincoln finally realized that what his son had suggested was in reality the right thing to do. Mrs. Lincoln was taken to a private hospital in Washington and the truth of her condition was kept from the public. Lincoln hoped that his wife's condition could be cured but, secretly he did not hold out much hope that treatment would be successful. Whatever happened, Lincoln vowed to see to it that his wife received the very best care that could be given regardless of the cost. They had endured too much together and she had been a good mother to their children, even if she had sometimes seemed cold and indifferent towards him. Besides, it was not in his nature to be anything less than the totally devoted husband and father.

Lincoln approached the podium and looked out over the crowd of faces that were now watching him. He could feel a certain amount of hostility and thought to himself, "It's been almost five years and there are still some that consider me the enemy. How do I make them see that the United States is no longer their enemy and that we want to see them succeed at making their nation work?" Lincoln thought about it for a moment and decided to deviate from his prepared comments at the last moment. He waited for the crowd to settle in and when it got quiet, he smiled at those in the front row who could see him well and took a deep breath and began the speech that he hoped would begin to heal the wounds that he could tell still existed.

He began by saying, "Ladies and Gentlemen, we are

gathered here to bear witness to a momentous event. The men that we honor today have a unique distinction that has only been witnessed on a rare occasion. That distinction is that they were instrumental in helping to found this country and now they have been chosen to lead it. Not since the time of George Washington has such a thing happened on this continent. They have proven themselves to be capable leaders on the battlefield and now, with the help of Almighty God, they will carry the same capability and tenacity into the future as leaders of this country. I have no doubt that they will be successful. They do, however face some very serious difficulties in the days ahead. In the interest of promoting a sense of goodwill between our countries, I have ordered Congress to appropriate the necessary resources to assist in establishing and maintaining a viable manufacturing industry here in the South." Anyone wishing to start a factory to manufacture goods will be eligible for assistance. I will appoint a liaison to work with President Lee's administration to see that anyone who applies for the assistance will be given full consideration."

There was a long silence after he made this statement and Lincoln was sure that he had failed in his attempt. Just as he was about to finish his speech, the crowd suddenly erupted with applause, whistles and chants of "Lincoln, Lincoln". He breathed a sigh of relief as he realized that once again, he had helped his nation turn a corner in history.

The celebration lasted four days. There were dinner parties, more speeches, and parades and of course, The President and Vice President spent time greeting citizens and shaking hands. At the end of the four-day celebration, President Lee and Vice President Longstreet found themselves reacting to a problem that they had found themselves in before. They were receiving daily reports of British ships off their coast that were harassing commercial ships bringing in goods for sale in the South.

Lee sent several very strongly worded letters to Queen Victoria protesting that the British ships were interfering in foreign commerce that they had no business being involved in. Lee's letters went largely ignored as if the British government was refusing to recognize the Confederacy even though all of their prior conditions for recognizing the new nation had now been met in full. It wasn't until they learned from former President Davis that there had been an attempt by the Crown to subvert several high ranking officers into a planned coup that they fully realized the gravity of the situation, Great Britain was now showing her true colors. She thought that she could regain possession of her lost colonies by driving a wedge between the two powers on the continent and then divide and conquer!

Lee thought to himself as he looked over the first intelligence reports of his presidency, "If they try to launch an attack against us, we are not yet recovered enough from the war to resist them for very long." He considered his options and then he walked to the Vice President's office and knocked on the door. Longstreet greeted his boss and offered him a chair.

Lee sat down in front of Longstreet's desk and, looking at his friend and now Vice President he said, "The British are going to attack us at some point because if they do and are successful, they can then threaten the United States and win back the North American continent. We must not let that happen. That would mean not only the end of this nation but the end of democracy on this continent."

Longstreet considered these last words and nodded solemnly. "What can we do, sir?" he asked.

Lee thought a moment and said, "Do you remember during the war how often we found ourselves outnumbered and in a bad tactical position?"

Longstreet nodded and said, "Don't remind me, I still have nightmares!"

Lee chuckled at the big man's attempt at dark humor. "Well, Peter, we are in a tight spot again and we shall have to do what we have always done at times like these, make the best use of the resources we have and bluff our way around the ones we don't have."

For the next hour and a half the two men sat behind the closed door of Longstreet's office and discussed the plan that had been taking shape in the mind of perhaps one of the greatest tactical generals since the likes of Julius Caesar and Alexander the Great. There was very little that the newly elected President of the Confederate States of

America had not thought of. But there were some small details and some refinements to his original ideas that Longstreet had come up with that proved without a doubt in the older man's mind that not only had Longstreet been a brilliant tactician and gifted general, but he was also the perfect man to hold his current position.

Several days later, it was reported in the local newspapers that there was an increase in activity in several of the military installations in and around Richmond. It was also noted that there seemed to be an increase in activity at the Tredegar Iron Works and several other manufacturing facilities that had been widely utilized to produce war materiel in the late war. Some speculated that this was an indication that there was trouble ahead for the fledgling nation. Those people had no idea how close to the truth they really were.

The increased activity had not escaped the notice of the Administration in the White House and even without the opinions of the press in Richmond they reached much the same conclusion. Realizing too that the fate of the Confederacy would also influence the fate of the United States, President Grant made certain arrangements and deployments. These deployments would not only strengthen his country's position and readiness but would also position resources in such a manner to lend support to the forces fielded by their Southern neighbors if, and when such support was needed and indeed asked for.

All of these things were noted by, and reported back to England by a small, highly skilled network of operatives who had been placed by the Crown to do exactly the job that they were now doing. By observing and reporting these activities back to England, they were providing the leaders there with the necessary information that they needed to properly and promptly react to the smallest breach in the new nation's security in order to capitalize on it and bring both of the upstart governments on the continent to ruin.

If this intelligence network had a strength it was that it relied heavily on the information provided by its operatives who were among the best the world had ever seen. If it had a weakness, it was that it relied heavily on the information provided by its operatives who, in this case had been drawn neatly into being used to send false information to their employers.

Because these observers were just that and not, in most cases, knowledgeable in complex military matters they simply took what they saw at face value and reported this back to England. The main problem with this was that they were reporting back exactly what the Confederate government wanted them to see. It was this sort of planning, diversion and pure luck that had dominated the Confederate Army's successes during the war and had now found a purpose afterwards—to help this young republic to survive one of the most critical periods in the life of any nation.

Based on information provided on current activities in both the United States and the Confederate States, it was determined that both nations were rapidly attempting to bring themselves to a state of readiness for another armed conflict. At the same time, there was much argument in Parliament and also at Buckingham Palace that perhaps a delay in mobilizing any forces was advisable. There were those who advocated swift and decisive movement by England but those voices were few and largely drowned out by the clamor for caution until it could be determined that such an invasion would be successful beyond doubt.

It was this level of caution that caused the British government to forestall its planned incursion onto the North American continent for the better part of three years, until events in the Confederacy revived hope in the notion that the plan could succeed. It was not until the fall of 1870 that the British monarchy could be convinced, albeit by a man whose loyalties were somewhat questionable, that the time to strike had come at last. A sign from on high had been received, he said. It was as if God himself was giving the word to commence operations. That sign was the sudden and unexpected death of the one man in whom the trust of an entire nation rested, the first President of the Confederacy elected by popular election, the man perhaps most of all was responsible for the existence of the Confederate nation in the first place. Robert E. Lee, beloved general, president, devoted husband and father had succumbed to a failing heart.

The news of Lee's death had spread like wildfire throughout Richmond and in turn throughout the South. Many Northern papers had picked up the story and were now scrambling to determine what effect that this would have on relations between their two countries. It also had many who were privy to information that had not been circulated to the general public wondering what Great Britain would do once they found out about this destabilizing event. Only time would tell how the British would react and, if the last three years had been enough time to prepare for the eventuality of that reaction.

CHAPTER 6
LAST RESPECTS
RICHMOND, VIRGINIA
OCTOBER 20, 1870

The weather was typical for an autumn day in the Capitol except that this anything but a typical autumn day. There was an oppressive air of sadness that hung over the city as if there were an impending storm. The area around the capitol building itself was a beehive of sullen activity. People came and went with deliberate steps in and out of the rotunda. Everyone was determined to get one last look at the man that had been so revered in not only Virginia but also the entire South. Parents took their children to gaze upon the face of a true hero.

The face was as familiar to the mourners as if it were a favorite family member—the regal bearing, the thick, wavy white hair and the neatly trimmed beard. The man's frame, almost six feet and his robust build at nearly two hundred pounds made him seem almost larger than life and it seemed to some that not even death could diminish the man who had become beloved by both soldiers and civilians. Here was the man who seemed to be the human embodiment of all that the Confederacy had fought to preserve. This was the funeral of a man whose name and deeds were legend but it was also the funeral of a Chief of State. The funeral was that of Robert E. Lee, gentleman, soldier, hero and second President of the Confederate States of America.

The rotunda of the Capitol building was, by all standards of the day a large room. However, today it could barely contain the pressing throngs of people who came to witness this once in a lifetime event. There was a subdued murmur of voices that seemed almost like some chanted prayer in a foreign tongue. In stark contrast to the almost ethereal mood and hushed tones of conversation surrounding the flag-draped coffin, there was an almost gaudy splash of colors all about the area. There was black crepe draped on the walls and around the coffin. Flags of various colors representing the member states of the Confederacy. The deep blue of the uniforms of the United States Army and the now standard gray uniform of the Confederate States Army as well as uniforms from other countries being worn by members of their country's diplomatic envoys to this somber event.

Most notably absent from the ranks of foreign dignitaries was the foreign minister from Great Britain. This owing to the increasing tensions between England and the two sovereign states that now comprised her former colonies. The difficulties between the three nation-states had their roots in the conflict that had resulted in the formation of the two nations that now occupied the major portion of the North American continent. During the late War Between the States, Great Britain had seen fit to station several regiments of Redcoats in the lower portions of Canada. The official explanation by then-Prime minister Lord Palmerston was due to the recent incursion of England's centuries old foe, the French into Mexico in 1862.

Her majesty, Queen Victoria, had thought that it was in the best interest of both the United States and England that there were troops nearby to lend a hand if Emperor Maxmillian's army got overly ambitious. Add to this the support given to the Confederacy during the hostilities as it became apparent to the Crown that the rebels had at least a fighting chance to succeed in its bid for independence.

For the Confederacy, England's duplicitous nature became apparent when, at a low point in that nation's fight to win her freedom, an attempt to subvert some of her more radical thinking military leaders into handing over control of large numbers of troops to help facilitate a military coup d'etat and install an administration more favorable to English domination of the fledgling nation. It was this tenuous relationship between the Old World and the New World that had now created a near war footing which none of the sides wanted or could afford but at the same time no one seemed able to stop their nation's slippery slide into the abyss.

It was that feeling of impending disaster that dominated

the thinking of nearly every person that came to pay their last respects to the man who, at the very outset of his country's quest for a national identity was probably the only person who fully understood what seeking that identity would demand and ultimately cost each and every person that lived to see it come about.

The rotunda of the Confederate Capitol building was already the scene of great commotion even before many of the key political figures ever made their appearances. There were men who had served under the General during the late war that had come out of a sense of duty to their former commander. There were the former slaves that had come to pay their respects to the man who had been so instrumental in giving them not only the freedom that they now enjoyed but also the chance to fight for the land that they loved beside those who had kept them in bondage for so many generations before.

On one side of the room nearest the funeral bier was a small grouping of seats that were there for use by the family of the deceased and also for persons of importance that came to lend emotional support to the family. Seated there now was Lee's youngest son, Robert E. Lee Jr. The young man bore the same noble features and bearing of his father but there was also a hint of the marks left behind by the physical and emotional scars that can only be wrought by long years of fighting and privation. It was his task at this time to be the representative of his family since his mother was by this time too frail and infirmed to attend owing to the ravages of arthritis that had left her wheelchair bound since the latter days of The War.

He was therefore somewhat elated to begin to see the familiar faces of those who had been closest to his father during the dark days of the War and in the days afterward when the elder Lee had been called back to the service of his country as its Chief Executive.

The first to arrive, as if by some unwritten rule of political protocol was the man that had not only served as Lee's closest aide and confidante during the war but as his Vice President and now President pro-tem, former Lieutenant General James Longstreet. The big man moved with a determined stride toward the coffin and, once there stood for a long moment gazing at the face of the man who was his superior but also held a place in Longstreet's heart reserved for a man who was as much beloved as a father. After a few moments the new President of the Confederacy turned and, making no attempt to hide his emotions, brushed aside a lone tear coursing down his cheek and moved to take a seat next to the General's son.

Taking Lee's hand in his own, spoke a quiet word of comfort, which elicited a smile from a son, bereft of a father. As the two men spoke in hushed tones, the very air of the room seemed to go completely still as all eyes in the room turned to see the next arrival at this most somber of occasions. Suddenly the room was abuzz with muted conversations, some of them in angry tones as the familiar face and tall angular frame of the former President of the United States, the man whom, for the entire South held at one time or another complete and utter contempt.

It was the arrival of Abraham Lincoln that almost caused the assembled masses to riot but for the memory of the man whom they had come to mourn and the latter's honest attempts during his presidency to see that the new nation was treated fairly and with compassion for all that it had suffered to gain its freedom. As Lincoln himself had said in his second inaugural address, "With malice toward none, with charity for all."

Longstreet leaned toward the young man seated at his side, said something inaudible to the crowd of mourners around them and rose to greet the former President. He strode forward and took Lincoln's large hand in his own and said "Thank you for coming Mr. President. I only wish we did not have to meet under such circumstances."

Lincoln nodded and said, " It would not have been proper to do otherwise. He gave so much of his life to both the United States and to the Confederacy; it would have been disrespectful not to come here to recognize that fact."

Longstreet nodded and paused briefly, trying to gather his thoughts and bolster his determination to follow through with his next statement. He adopted a formal stance and in his best "political" voice said, "Mr. President, I am hosting a state dinner tonight at the Executive Residence. I would be honored sir, if you would consent to attend."

"It would be both an honor and a privilege." Lincoln said. "I am staying at the Spotswood Hotel."

Longstreet said to the former chief executive, "Sir, it would be my great pleasure if you would consent to spend the remainder of your stay at the Executive Residence."

Lincoln smiled and said "Mr. President, there is nothing that I would enjoy more. I shall have my bags ready when your man comes to pick me up."

Longstreet thanked Lincoln for accepting the invitation and promised to see him later that evening and then he went back to young Robert's side. He said to him, "Robert, Mr. Hood and I were discussing what was going to happen to you and your family now that your father is gone. Mr. Hood has said that he wishes to speak to you on a matter of some importance in this regard. I suggest that you listen to what he has to say and do not dismiss him out of hand. He had a great deal of respect for your father, as did we all and it is partially out of that respect and also partially because you have proven yourself to be a capable man that he wants to deal with you on this."

The young man smiled a sad smile and said, "Very well Mr. President, I shall listen to what Mr. Hood has to say and will not make any rash decisions."

With his task of inviting all of the principals to dinner done, Longstreet went forward toward the bier and taking a last look at the face of the man who meant so much to not only Longstreet but the entire South as well, turned and made his way out of the Capitol rotunda and down the steps to summon his coach and make the trip back to the Executive Mansion so that he could begin to organize and orchestrate this colossal event which every head of state around the world seemed to enjoy but one which causes all of them to secretly dread.

Tonight would be a mixture of old times remembered, and new beginnings that may well decide whether his country would stand or fall. Longstreet prayed a silent prayer that all would go well. He had no idea just how well things were going to go but if he had to guess, he did not hold much hope for a peaceful co-existence now that Lee, the great strategist and leader were no longer here to maintain the delicate balance between politics, policy, strategy and common sense.

CHAPTER 7

REMEMBRANCES

THE EXECUTIVE MANSION, RICHMOND

The guests all began to arrive at a few minutes past seven o'clock that evening. First to arrive, owing to the close proximity of their residence to the Executive mansion, were General Jackson and his wife Anna. General Jackson was resplendent in his finest uniform with all of its gold braid and numerous medals from campaigns past. Mrs. Jackson was as beautiful as Longstreet could ever remember seeing her but tonight there was something different about her. She seemed to radiate a sort of ethereal energy, which Longstreet could not identify. He greeted them warmly and escorted them personally to the large sitting room just off the formal dining room. After his guests were comfortably seated and refreshments were distributed he engaged them in small talk to pass the time before his other guests arrived. He could not get over the feeling that there was something especially important about this evening, even the General was behaving like someone who had just been told a great secret and was anxious to find someone in whom to confide.

Just as Longstreet was about to inquire as to the Jackson's strange mood, the doorman announced the next arrival. With a great deal of fanfare, Pickett, Stuart and Hood all arrived at the same moment as if they had been together all evening. The trio entered the sitting room and after exchanging pleasantries, Hood spoke to Longstreet in his usual gruff Texas manner saying, "Well Pete, the deed is done! I have offered young Robert a position as manager of my interests here in Richmond and after much goading and pressure on my part and the part of my two companions here, he has reluctantly agreed to take the position. The salary I have offered him is slightly pretentious but nothing short of what the young man is worth. Remember what he did with that battery back during the battle of…Oh, hell I can't remember which one it was but you yourself know that he wound up being almost as good an artillery commander as Ol' Porter Alexander himself. And if you will remember how good HE was, you know that that is no small feat. I have no doubt young Robert will show the same aptitude and drive in this new endeavor and he will be able to divert his mind from his current troubles and I will make a tidy profit in the bargain."

At this Longstreet chuckled. He always knew that his friend from Texas was shrewd but he was gaining a new respect for just how shrewd he really was. Pickett entered the room and upon seeing Anna Jackson there swept the hat from his head and with a bow that would have made a courtier jealous said, "My dear Mrs. Jackson it is a pleasure to once again find myself in your sublime presence."

At this Anna blushed and slapped playfully at her husband who was grinning like a schoolboy and pinching at her cheeks saying, "My dearest *esposita,* I do believe that the General is trying to win your affections away from me."

At the mere mention of such a thing, Pickett straightened up to his full height. Adopting an air of feigned offense said to his superior, "Sir, you slight me. At turns you accuse me of desiring to cause pain to one of my dearest and oldest friends and at the same time you assume that this lovely creature would ever be swayed by a honeyed tongue to turn her back on the man who loves her more than he loves his own life. And that, I can assure you, would never happen! Mrs. Jackson is without a doubt the most devoted wife that any man could ever have."

As if to lend credence to his words, Pickett strode forward and first offered his friend/commander a crisp, perfectly executed salute followed by taking him by the hand and vigorously shaking it as though he were at a pump attempting to prime it to draw water. After much laughter all around, General Stuart, walking with his now familiar stilted gait approached his former commander and his friends and smiling a smile that was almost reminiscent of his former days, but not quite, he said, "

Well aren't we a group? Here is the one man who never aspired to anything higher than the rank of a Corps commander and look at him now, Commander-in-chief of the entire Confederate Army and Navy. And then there is George here, Chief of Military Intelligence. *INTELLIGENCE?* Oh well, I guess you have to go with what you have to work with!"

At this, Pickett's face took on a look of surprise that few had ever seen. Just as he was about to demand an explanation and an apology, Stuart let go with a belly laugh that few people who had not known him before would have ever thought he could have mustered. At this the whole room filled with laughter at the plight suffered by Pickett who, good naturedly shrugged off the whole incident.

Just as things were settling down the doorman reappeared and announced the next visitors saying, "Mr. President, President and Mrs. Grant, former President Lincoln and Governor and Mrs. Chamberlain have just arrived."

The astonished looks from his other guests spoke volumes to Longstreet. First there was the disbelief that he would ever invite "those people" into his country's executive mansion followed by the realization that here was an opportunity to discover some information that the men assembled here did not have available at a time when it would have proven most useful. Little did they realize just how much was to be discovered and how much they themselves might actually divulge to their former antagonists. Longstreet turned just in time to see the Grants, Chamberlains, & Lincoln enter the sitting room.

Grant was dressed conservatively but neatly in a dark suit, Mrs. Grant wore a simple but elegant evening dress that was entirely appropriate for a woman of her age. Governor Chamberlain moved slowly and gingerly as if walking on a floor of glass. Longstreet thought to himself, as most of the other men did, "This man is truly amazing. Only someone with an incredible will to live would have survived the injuries that he sustained and managed any kind of normal life and here he is not only leading a normal life but leading his state's government as well."

With no attempt at concealing his admiration and concern for his guest's plight, Longstreet called to his staff and had a large, overstuffed chair brought into the sitting room specifically to allow his injured guest to be comfortable. Upon seeing this display Grant remarked, "It is well that we in positions of influence should learn to put our past differences behind us and show compassion to each other for what we have all been through."

Longstreet nodded thoughtfully and said, "We should strive to do more and endeavor never to do less, to paraphrase General Lee."

At this the group looked at each other, suddenly remembering the event that had brought them together in the first place. After Governor Chamberlain was seated and made as comfortable as possible, the rest of the party seated themselves around the room and made small talk until it was time for dinner. The dining room was smaller than that in the White House, a fact that was commented on by Lincoln saying, "Your dining room is much better suited for these types of affairs Mr. President. I always thought that the formal dining room in the White House to be much too large to allow the guests to enjoy each other's company. It was sort of like having a picnic in the barn!"

The guests all had a good laugh at the former president's joke and each noted to themselves that he seemed to be genuinely enjoying himself. The truth was that the current Chief Executive knew he had never enjoyed the affairs hosted during his administration, as much for the politicking and flesh pressing as the fact that if he had ever been actually enjoying himself, his wife would have been at his elbow to roundly scold him for his "Backwoods Behavior" as she put it. Grant made a mental note to check into the rumors that, after the Lincolns had left office and had suffered the loss of young Tad from pleurisy, Mary Lincoln had become distraught and had increasingly begun to lose touch with reality. Only after much cajoling from their eldest son Robert, Lincoln had his wife committed to a mental institution in Maryland with instructions that she should never want for anything but that she also never be allowed to leave that facility.

Whatever the reason for the former President's newly found ability to relax and enjoy himself, Grant thought, "good for him, after what he went through with the War and the assassination attempt by that no-account actor Booth, the man was entitled to a little bit of happiness."

It was while he was involved in these musings that someone mentioned the fact that they had noticed that Robert Lee had not arrived as planned. Longstreet called to one of the staff and asked that he go and inquire after the young man. About thirty minutes had gone by when the man returned and informed the gathering that, "Young mister Lee begs the forgiveness of the guests at his total lack of courtesy in this manner but that after the events of the past few days, he is in dreadful shape and desires nothing more at this time than a few days of rest to steady himself for the days yet to come."

They all nodded at this and some voiced genuine concern for not only the young man's health but also his state of mind. At this, Longstreet once again addressed the man, who had been his courier for the evening and said, "Go to Mr. Lee's residence and give him our regards. Tell him that I have instructed you to attend to whatever he needs. If he desires of anything, you will provide it and make whatever financial arrangements necessary to have the debt satisfied through this office. If he desires to be left alone and not be disturbed, you will post yourself outside his door and see that he is not disturbed until such time that he seeks contact with the rest of the world."

The man nodded grimly and turned on his heel to go. He was just about to reach the door when General Jackson stepped up to the man who unconsciously adopted a position of attention at the general's approach. Jackson looked the man over from head to toe for a brief moment and said simply, "Name, rank and regiment."

There were surprised looks from all in attendance at this seeming confrontation. The man's reaction was almost imperceptible except to those who had seen it a hundred times or more before. "Addison, Lester, First Sergeant, late of the 33rd Virginia Infantry Regiment, "Stonewall's Brigade"." At this, a cloud passed briefly over the general's face before he issued the command, "Carry on First Sergeant".

At this the man did a crisp about face and left the house. When Jackson turned around, he found himself looking into the astonished faces of the guests. When asked how he knew that the man had been in the army, Jackson simply said, "He moved like my old foot cavalry."

When asked what had caused his expression to change at the mention of "Stonewall's Brigade", Jackson replied, "I have never liked that name associated with myself. I have always thought that the name belonged to the men not their leader."

The group nodded their understanding of the man's lack of desire for ostentatious titles and sobriquets. After dinner the guests moved back into the sitting room where the women began talking amongst themselves in hushed tones and the men moved closer to the fireside and availed themselves of brandy and cigars. The former was a gift from Hood to his former commander. The latter was acquired courtesy of President Grant who long ago had gotten the reputation of being quite a connoisseur of fine cigars and who, during his tenure as General-in-Chief of the Union Army had established an unofficial supply line for the support of his affinity for them.

He had somehow managed to maintain contact with people who had access to those wonderfully mellow, hand-rolled cigars from the island of Cuba. Although of late, Grant found that he did not enjoy them as much as he had in the past. He attributed this to his advancing years and the stresses imposed upon him as President. He and Longstreet talked of future cooperative efforts between the United States and the Confederacy saying, "Since we are to be neighbors, I think that it would be a good idea for us to build a gate in the fence between us so that we may support each other and therefore promote stability on the North American continent."

Longstreet nodded his approval of this idea and said, "I only wish that this had been possible five years ago!"

Each man nodded in assent to this when the subject turned to the fortunes of each of them and of their friends that they fought with and against in that struggle. Each man related stories about their involvement and provided their listeners with perspectives that most knew little or nothing at all about. Longstreet spoke about his involvement with the Gettysburg Campaign, which was one that had involved every man in the room save Grant. Grant voiced a question that unbeknownst to him would begin a journey of discovery for them all and had the potential to make or break the fledgling nation in her struggle to prove to the world that this country could and would make it as a viable member of the international community.

He simply said to the men gathered around him, "Tell me about Gettysburg." The other men looked at each other and shared a moment of inner reflection that asked the question, "Do I really want to go back there, even if it is just in my mind? What hidden dangers are there in bringing this all back up again?

After what seemed like an eternity, Longstreet, staring into his brandy, spoke almost in a whisper saying, "I lost some good men and some good friends in that fight."

The other men who had been participants nodded and said quietly, "Damn fine men...on both sides."

Longstreet continued speaking saying, "If it hadn't been for Harry Heth's boys looking for shoes, we might never have had that fight. How were we to know that Buford's cavalry had already come through the town and were waiting on us to show up?"

At this, Pickett and Hood looked at Stuart who was suddenly very quiet and had his eyes cast toward the floor. When he looked up, there was a look of an old wound that had suddenly festered and re-opened. They all noticed that it appeared that the young General was on the verge of tears when he finally spoke up, his voice trembling, saying, "I never thought for a single moment that I was letting you all down. All our reports were that their army was miles from any point on the map with any type of military value. Besides, we came as fast as we could after the couriers found us north of Rockville."

Longstreet, who had commanded an entire Corps in Lee's Army of Northern Virginia, said to Stuart, "We're glad that you showed up when you did. Your arrival, Hood's flanking maneuver at Devil's Den and the unexpected arrival of Jackson's foot cavalry, which poised itself between Meade's army and Washington City was that combination of events that led to the Peace Conference in Baltimore, which gave the Confederacy an upper hand at being able to determine its own destiny."

Lincoln smiled at their reference to the conference. He said, "Yes sir, you folks had me over a barrel that day! Stanton and the rest of the Cabinet were beside themselves with apoplexy when they realized that we were going to have to let the Southern states go their own way. They all were positive that you posed a perpetual threat to our borders. It took a lot of convincing for me to get them to believe that all you folks wanted was to be left alone to run your own affairs, and since your Congress and President Davis had abolished slavery just a few months into the war they really didn't have anything left to squawk about!"

They all chuckled at the thought of Lincoln's former Secretary of War, a War Democrat and fierce opponent of slavery, being suddenly left without a motive for prosecuting the war. Lincoln continued his description of the feeling in Washington during this time. He said, "What was particularly disturbing to some folks in the Capitol in those days were the reports coming back from the battlefields in '62 & '63 of the sudden appearance of hordes of Negro soldiers, in GRAY uniforms! General Fremont had always advocated the enlistment of colored troops. I guess you folks just beat him to the punch."

With that, the assembled Confederate commanders all nodded and Jackson said, "Our 1st and 2nd Independent Colored Infantry Regiments really played hell with your troops during the Seven Days and Wilderness campaigns. Bedford Forrest never believed that you could make good soldiers out of them. Boy, they sure proved him wrong!"

At that everyone in the room nodded agreement. Grant turned to Longstreet and said, "If your current groups of Negro troops are performing as well as our 9th and 10th Cavalry and 25th and 26th Infantry regiments, you have a fine group of soldiers."

Longstreet said, "They are indeed Mr. President. In fact, we have integrated them into our Navy as well. They are proving to be tough, reliable and capable in whatever jobs they are assigned. I would put any of our soldiers, sailors and marines, black or white up against any armed force in the world today."

Grant smiled at Longstreet's enthusiasm for his troops and said "Well sir, I hope that it will never come to that. But if it does, rest assured that the United States government will lend whatever aid and assistance it can whenever it is requested."

At these words everyone in the room including the former president of the United States turned and with an astonished look regarded Grant's face. Everyone could see that the man was totally serious at the offer to assist his country's former foe. Hood, Jackson and Pickett searched each other's faces for a moment and then with a wide grin, Pickett voiced the unspoken thought that he had shared with his former comrades-in-arms and said, "Well, I guess I have lived long enough to see everything now! Mr. President, if I were you I would take President Grant up on his most generous offer. If he is half as good at being President as he was at being a General, then together there is no military force on the planet that we cannot defeat!"

Grant colored slightly at the compliment paid by his former adversary, Mrs. Grant fairly beamed. Chamberlain, who had been mostly silent throughout the exchange, finally spoke up saying, "General Pickett, he has indeed proven an able President even though there are some in his Cabinet whose motives are somewhat suspect. I can assure you that he is a man totally above reproach.

The color in Grants cheeks deepened at the further compliments. He finally spoke up and said, "Gentlemen, there is such a thing as gilding the lily a bit too much. I have simply tried to surround myself with people who are able to do the things that I cannot do myself or that possess certain knowledge that I myself do not. I am only sorry that Governor Chamberlain did not accept my offer as Secretary of State. I am sure that a man of his education, loyalty and fierce determination would have made an excellent addition to my cabinet."

Now it was Chamberlain's turn to blush at the high praise received from his country's Chief Executive. At that moment, the familiar face and gravelly voice of his late Sergeant and close confidante 'Buster' Kilrane who died from wounds received on Little Round Top came to him and the thought, "I didn't do everything right or else Buster would still be alive today". At this thought a wistful look clouded his face. Fannie looked at her husband and said, "Mr. President, your offer to my husband was most gracious and greatly appreciated but, I am afraid that it is I who is to blame for Lawrence's refusal. I worried so about him when he went off to fight, and when he was wounded at Fredericksburg and then again at Gettysburg we feared we might lose him. I made myself a promise that if God spared his life, I would do everything in my power to keep him from doing anything that would cause him too much stress and aggravate his wounds. After his tenure at Bowdoin College I thought that he would settle into a quiet life of retirement. I guess that I should have known him better than that. When he was approached to run for Governor of Maine, I tried to dissuade him but he pleaded and cajoled until I had no other recourse but to relent and allow him to follow his heart just as I had done in 1861."

Chamberlain looked at his wife and everyone in the room saw the look of total devotion to each other in their faces. They thought, "Here are two people perfectly matched one to the other." Julia Grant took the opportunity to voice her sympathy to Fannie's position saying, "My dear I know just how you feel. And even though he was not seriously wounded as your dear husband was, it never left my mind that the same fate might await him at any moment. In his Army career I got used to his long absences but that was peacetime and the threat of danger was remote. But when the war broke out we were living in Galena and Lys was working in his father's shop. When the first reports of fighting came in, I could see that he wanted to go, get back into uniform and perform whatever service his country required of him. I couldn't keep him from it. It would have made him miserable. Sometimes you just have to let them go and hope for the best."

Fannie smiled at the older woman with an understanding smile and thought to herself, "Here is a kindred spirit. I must make an effort to get to know her better."

Grant smiled at his wife's relating of this most private of moments, knowing that this was not her usual manner and that she was attempting to set the younger woman's mind at ease about her husband's desire at public service. The conversation then turned to a more serious note when Longstreet turned to Grant and said, "The British have tried to subvert our government and our military. I fear that they may try something more overt in the future. I would like your assurances Mr. President that you and your government will not aid them in this endeavor."

Grant nodded seriously and said, "Yes, I had heard about the attempted coup. They tried to get some of your high-ranking officers to march on the Confederate White House and overthrow President Davis. I can't honestly say that the results might have favored a quick Union victory but it is possible. The only problem then would have had to have been facing a re-constituted Confederate army supported by British troops and armed with British arms. All in all I am glad the attempt failed. Were you ever able to identify those officers that participated in the plot?"

Longstreet nodded and said, "It turns out that Sir Arthur Fremantle was here as something more than an advisor/observer. He managed to enlist the aid of two of our general officers and several field grade officers. We caught him meeting with them and after several hours of intense interrogation, convinced him of the folly of his endeavor. We obtained a complete roster of the officers involved, deported Fremantle, and quietly rounded up the officers involved."

Grant's face showed a puzzled look at this. He said, "I never heard about any trials or any punishments being meted out. What ever happened to the conspirators?"

Longstreet sighed and said, "We didn't want word to get out to the troops that there ever was any type of takeover attempt. We called the officers involved to Richmond and quietly arrested them when they arrived. We identified the 'ring leaders' and those men were taken to a remote location and shot under the Articles of War for espionage. The rest of the officers involved...you will appreciate the irony of this...were imprisoned in Libby prison right here in Richmond. Two hung themselves in their cells and the rest are quietly serving their sentences as we speak."

At the mention of men serving prison sentences for espionage during the war still imprisoned five years later, Grant asked, "How long were they sentenced to serve?"

Longstreet's face grew grim and he simply said, "How long would you imprison a man convicted of trying to hand over your country to a foreign power?"

Grant nodded his understanding that the men would never again be free. Fannie Chamberlain looked at her husband, who was also nodding his understanding of the situation and asked, "What does he mean Lawrence?"

Chamberlain answered his wife saying, "Those men will never leave Libby prison as long as they are alive and rightly so."

She put her hand to her mouth in surprise and gasped, "Merciful Heaven!"

Grant sat shaking his head saying, "Who would have believed that we would imprison our own people for attempting to overthrow the government our fathers and grandfathers fought to create and preserve? It sort of makes you wonder why we fought our war!"

Grant then turned to Jackson and said, "General, how is it that you came to be in the vicinity of Gettysburg during that fateful time? I had heard rumors that you had died! And I must tell you, and please forgive me for the thought, that at the moment that I heard the news of your 'death' part of me said, "Thank God, now we might actually be able to win this war!" How did you keep an entire enemy nation completely ignorant of your movements and your intentions?"

At the mention of the ruse that helped his country win the right to self determination, Jackson simply smiled one of his trademark, thin, humorless smiles and said, "It all started one day at the Corbin house on Moss Neck near Chancellorsville. I had been feeling a bit run down and tired and was going to see my physician, Dr. Maguire who examined me and gave me the most frightening diagnosis that I think I have ever received."

He said, "General, you have an advanced case of pneumonia and it is strictly by the grace of God that you are able to last long enough to come to see me. No matter, there is only one effective treatment for pneumonia and that is bed rest and oil of camphor to open up your chest and get rid of the fluid building up in your lungs even as we speak. So against my better judgment I allowed myself to be taken to hospital and there I spent the next month undergoing a series of new and experimental treatments. The results were that the pneumonia cleared up and I was able to rejoin my Corps and assist General Lee in planning a little surprise for the Federals who it looked might be trying to occupy Gettysburg and plan a little surprise of their own.

We were able to move from Moss Neck, up the York/ James peninsula and through Winchester and managed to keep our movements screened by the Blue Ridge Mountains. By the time Meade realized what had happened, we were between him and Washington!"

Pickett joined the conversation at that point and gave his impression of what happened on that day. "I received orders from General Lee through General Longstreet to make a demonstration against the Union center and that was as much information that I had up to that point. I never dreamed that they had planned for Hood to continue around the right and up over the top of the hill to threaten the Union positions in Devil's Den and Cemetery Ridge."

Chamberlain smiled at this and said, "How do you think my men and I felt when you started up that hill? You came on screaming like some type of fiend that I had a hard time controlling my men and keeping them from running. Luckily, by the time your men had reached the breastworks, my men fell back to their rallying positions. It wasn't much time but we managed to spoil your little party."

He continued by saying, "General Jackson, I seem to remember hearing that one of your staff was killed the evening following the first day's fighting around the

Chancellor House. What was he doing out that late in the evening and so far forward of your lines?"

Jackson's face took on a pained expression when he thought about the young lieutenant that fell in his place. He himself had planned to ride out and scout the forward area to determine the enemy's disposition and it was that same afternoon when he went to Dr. Maguire to complain of a shortness of breath that was the telltale symptom of pneumonia. When young Marshall had come to him for orders, Jackson considered telling him to have the rest of the staff stand down and await his return. But a desperate need for intelligence as to the Federal army's disposition took precedence over his desire to see his staff well rested for the days following. It was therefore a quirk of fate that the young Lieutenant Marshall was riding at the front of the group when they passed within hearing distance of a group of men from the 18th North Carolina Infantry who thinking it to be Federal cavalry opened fire on the group with their outdated .69 caliber smoothbore muskets.

These were not terribly accurate but at 50-75 yards were accurate enough to score some telling hits especially since the men loaded them with a lethal combination of a large round ball and 3 pieces of buckshot affectionately referred to as "buck and ball". It was 3 such loads propelled by their 70 grain black powder charge that quite literally swept the young Lieutenant from the saddle, dead before his body even fell to the earth. Jackson mourned the young man's death with the same depth of feeling that a father would show for a favored son.

He had the young man's body prepared and shipped home to his parents at his own expense. His chief of staff Alexander 'Sandie' Pendleton, son of General Lee's chief of artillery, escorted the body home. When he met with the boy's parents, he gave them a letter, written by the general extolling the many virtues of their son and expressing the profound sense of loss that he himself felt at having the young man snatched so cruelly and senselessly away from all who knew and loved him.

Jackson promoted the young man posthumously to the rank of Major and made certain that a request for a survivor's pension at that rank was approved by no less than General Lee himself and was forwarded to President Davis for his personal signature, thereby assuring that the young man's parents would never be in need during their declining years when they would have depended on the boy for their well being.

When Grant heard all of this he said with a great deal of sadness, "A great many young men lost their lives during that war and the world is poorer for it. It will never be known what great deeds they may have done or what vital service they might have performed had they lived."

All in the room nodded silently at the President's observation. Finally the evening drew to a close and the guests began to take their leave of their host. Among the last to leave was General Pickett. As the last of the guests shook hands all around and departed the Executive mansion, Longstreet looked at his old friend and said,

"George, what's clawing at your gut? You've been stalking around this evening like you were about to jump right out of your skin if somebody would have said, 'BOO'. What's on your mind?"

Pickett looked quickly around to make sure that all of the staff were well out of earshot and said, "There is something that you need to know about Mr. President, something that only your predecessor and I knew anything about. Something so top secret that he swore me to secrecy and said that even you, his Vice President need not know."

At this last revelation, Longstreet's face took on a puzzled and irritated look. Seeing this, Pickett told his friend, "I am sorry Pete I wanted to tell you but the old man made me swear not to tell you. He said that the decision to go ahead with the project and the decision to use it should be the responsibility of only one man. He said that way if anything went wrong or public opinion went against him, you would be held blameless and would escape any political backlash that would prevent you from keeping your job and thereby allowing you to help speed up the healing process in the country. In any event, all that is moot now. You are the President now and as such you need to have this information so that you can determine what to do with it and if and when to put the plans in motion."

Saying this, Pickett sat on the settee next to his old friend and now his superior and began relating to him the substance of a plan that had been two years in the planning and execution. That plan was now nearing completion and Longstreet listened, dumbstruck to the details of an ambitious plan to provide a measure of security to his country that did not at this time exist.

Meanwhile, in a carriage bound for the Spottswood Hotel, the Grants, Chamberlains and Lincoln were busy discussing the evening's events. Grant said to the other two men, "This has been a very informative evening. I always knew Longstreet to be a capable soldier but I did not realize that he had become such an adept politician."

Chamberlain and Lincoln nodded their agreement to the President's assessment of his counterpart. Lincoln was silent for a moment and then turning to the other men said, "He seems to be handling the transition of power remarkably well under the circumstances. It will be interesting to see how he handles his military. Those gentlemen are some of the finest military leaders on the North American continent. If he's not careful, he could wind up facing a military takeover."

At the mention of this Grant shot Chamberlain a look as if to say, "Do you think they might try it?" Chamberlain looked at his President and gave him a look in response that for all intents and purposes could have meant, "I suppose it's possible, but likely? I don't think so." With this silent exchange, Grant came to a decision with regard to their neighbor to the South.

He now announced to the passengers in the carriage

that decision. "I think we have an opportunity here. If the Confederacy is attacked either from within or without, I think it would be in our best interest to assist President Longstreet in any way that we can."

Both men regarded the Chief Executive with a look of amazement. Grant was showing some of the cunning and tenacity that had won him fame on battlefields from Chapultepec to Ft. Donelson and Appomattox. Lincoln turned to Grant and said, "You may want to start taking stock of what military resources you have considering that you may be called upon to use them at a moment's notice."

Grant nodded and said, "I have already begun. The only thing that I am not sure of is who will lead the troops. We have plenty of fine officers for a peacetime army but many of the officers that served in the war are either dead or were so severely wounded that they are unable to take the field. I suppose we could accelerate the graduation of the cadet class at West point which would give us some qualified junior officers but we need men with experience that aren't too old or busted up to take the field."

He turned to Chamberlain and said, "I sure could use you right now Lawrence. Would you consider serving as a staff officer in Washington? Not exactly the type of duty that garners a man medals and glory, but you've already got enough of those that if you ever fell into the Potomac in uniform, they'd carry you straight to the bottom!" He chuckled.

At this, Mrs. Grant shot her husband a withering stare while Fannie Chamberlain's face showed the worry of being the wife of a military commander. He looked at his wife and said to Grant, "I will serve my country in whatever capacity she needs me. If Fannie will consent to move to Washington with me so that we can be together, I will accept your offer."

Grant now turned to Fannie and said, "My dear, it seems that you outrank me! I promise you that the job that I have in mind for your husband will not tax his health in the least and he would only be in danger if the enemy marched down Pennsylvania Avenue."

At this Fannie smiled and said in her most gracious voice, belying her internal turmoil, "Very well Mr. President, I shall let you borrow my husband with the understanding that I get him back when all of this is over."

Grant smiled at Mrs. Grant and said, "Well my dear, it looks as though you shall have someone to have tea with in the afternoons and who will sit up with you worrying in the wee hours of the night!"

Julia Grant swatted at her husband with her fan and said, "You mind what I say Lys, you send that boy back safe and sound to his family or else you'll answer to me!"

Grant rolled his eyes in mock horror and said, "Oh dear, perish the thought that I should EVER disobey a direct order from you!"

Everyone in the carriage laughed the tense laugh of people who were uncertain of the future. Lincoln spoke up and said, "I place myself at your disposal Mr. President. If I can be of some small help, you have only to ask."

Grant glanced at his companions and then said to the tall man from Illinois, "I would be honored to have whatever advice and help that you feel compelled to give."

At that moment, Chamberlain spoke up and said, "Whom do you have in mind for your overall Cavalry commander?

At this question, Grant thought a moment and said, "I really don't know. I would have liked to have had Custer for the job but what with all the publicity surrounding him at the moment, I don't think that it would be a good idea."

Lincoln nodded his understanding of the situation and Chamberlain's face wore a look of disgust. Both Julia Grant and Fannie Chamberlain regarded their husbands as if expecting some explanation and when none came, Mrs. Grant turned to her husband and asked, "What publicity Lys? I don't believe that I have seen anything in the papers about anything concerning the 'Boy General'. What has he done?"

A pained look passed across Grant's face, knowing that his wife would continue to inquire and would not be satisfied with less than a full explanation. He looked at his predecessor and then at the Chamberlains. Fannie wore an expression on her face similar to that, which was now displayed on the face of the First Lady. After getting tacit nods from the other men in the carriage Grant took a deep breath. Expelling half of it as if preparing to fire a shot from a rifle, Grant began to explain why Custer, the young man who became a Brigadier General at just 21 during the war and was now a Colonel with a brevet of Major General just shy of his 29th birthday, could not and would not be her husband's choice for overall command of the Cavalry forces of his country.

CHAPTER 8
DISCOVERIES

Longstreet stared at his Chief of Military Intelligence with a look of incredulity. He had just been told about his nation's efforts at building a weapon to maintain the security of its borders that was so secret that the Vice President was not even informed of its existence. Longstreet's emotions ran the gamut from surprise and astonishment to disbelief and anger, however brief at the man who had ordered that this important piece of information be kept from him. He had followed that man for almost three years through some of the fiercest and bloodiest fighting he had ever seen and in that time had developed a trust for Lee that translated itself into a feeling of devotion that, if it had been ordered, would have obliged Longstreet to charge Hell itself.

Finally, after listening to Pickett for what seemed like hours, Longstreet asked the foremost questions in his mind in rapid succession, almost too fast for Pickett to gauge his Commander-in-Chief's mood. Longstreet said, "Alright George, now that you've told me WHAT it is and WHERE it's being built, can you also tell me WHEN it will be ready to be put into service?"

Pickett ignored his friend's irritated mood and chalked it up to the sudden stress of being thrust into the Presidency, the lateness of the hour, the loss of a good and trusted friend and then the sudden revelation that that friend was less than truthful on a matter that to Longstreet at least seemed of paramount importance to the safety and security of the fragile Confederate States of America.

Pickett tried to deflect some of Longstreet's irritation with some of his well-known and much maligned aloof humor saying, "Why Mr. President, what kind of Chief of Intelligence would I be if I didn't at least know that?"

Feigning a hurt and dejected look on his face at the moment he said this must have been just the right touch because suddenly he saw some of the old light come to his friend's face and then Longstreet broke into a broad grin and chuckled saying, "I suppose you're right George. So tell me, when can we expect this 'thing' to be ready to be put to use and how do you recommend we proceed?"

At this, Pickett smiled at the President and said, "She's ready now sir, but I have conferred with Major Dixon and we are in agreement sir, that she should not be deployed but held in reserve, hidden until such time as she is needed."

Longstreet nodded and thought the counsel to be a wise one since he knew Pickett personally and had been assured by many who knew the man that Major Dixon was not a man who rushed into anything and could always be counted on to think a situation through thoroughly before acting on his decisions. Longstreet thought a moment then said, "Very well George, we'll leave her where she is for the moment, Just be sure that you have the ability to get her going with a minimum of effort in as short a time as possible."

Pickett nodded seriously and said, "I have already seen to it, sir. We are keeping the crew quartered at the site and there is a contingent of Marines providing security. No one will know about this that we don't tell. We can have her under way in 20-30 minutes."

Longstreet clapped his old friend on the shoulder and said, "I don't care what Hood says, you ARE the best choice for Chief of Military Intelligence that I could have hoped for. The General sure knew how to pick the right man for the job, God rest him!"

At the same moment, the Grants, the Chamberlains and former President Lincoln were deeply engaged in a lively discussion about Grant's first choice for overall command of the Cavalry forces of the United States. Both Fannie Chamberlain and Julia Grant were sitting in utter shock at what they had just been told. Fannie asked the question that was on everyone's mind saying, "If he was romantically involved with the wife of one of his subordinates and he was caught *in flagrante dilecto* by the woman's husband, I don't blame him for trying to kill the man. The fact that he survived the shooting not withstanding, why on Earth has he not been cashiered from the service?"

Mrs. Grant nodded in agreement. Grant said, "Mrs. Chamberlain, you don't exactly court martial a war hero and winner of his nation's highest award for valor on this kind of thing. Its bad publicity for the service, the government, and not to mention the man himself. He was hospitalized for months after the shooting. Apparently the woman's husband is a crack shot with a pistol and it is only by the grace of God that the man was not killed outright."

At this last statement Julia Grant snorted, "If you ask me, he should have been killed. He not only jeopardized that young woman's life and marriage, which I can only assume is over. But he also betrayed the love and devotion of a woman who fairly idolizes her husband. I mean, did you see the letter that she sent to the editor of the Washington Post after the accusations of misconduct that were leveled against her husband by some of the officers that he commanded at Fort Hastings in the Dakota Territory? They said that he was brutal not only to captured Indians but to his men as well. From the letter that Libby Custer wrote to the editor of the Washington Post, you would have thought that she was going to start going door to door at every senator's house and take scalps!"

Grant and Lincoln glanced at each other and gave a knowing look that said that Mrs. Grant had hit the nail on the head with her summary of the situation. Fannie and Lawrence Chamberlain were only slightly less convinced of the guilt and rightness of the calamities that had befallen Custer. Finally, Chamberlain spoke up and said, "Too bad we don't have Buford around anymore. He was a damn fine horse soldier and a damn fine man. He would have been perfect for the job."

At the mention of Buford's name, Grant and Lincoln both nodded remembering the man that had held Thoroughfare gap and had held the Confederate advance on Gettysburg, only to succumb to injuries received almost a year before. But suddenly, Grant had a moment of inspiration. If he couldn't have Buford, then at least he could have someone that had been with Buford and had become a fine Cavalry officer in his own right.

Grant looked at Lincoln and then at Chamberlain and said, "What about General Devin? Is he fit to command? He was with Buford and learned a great deal from the man. Can he do it?"

The two looked at each other and then Chamberlain said, "Might be our best hope Mr. President. You might want to send for him when we get back to Washington."

Grant stared out the carriage window for a moment and then looked at the others and said, "Well, that takes care of the Cavalry, now we just need to find a capable field commander for the Infantry and the Artillery."

At this, Lincoln advised his successor by saying, "You'll also need a capable naval officer to run things on the water. You never know who or what might try that approach."

Grant thought about this for a moment and then said, "We'll have to do some checking around and ask some experts whom they would suggest. Mr. President, are you still in Dutch with Mr. Ericsson?"

At the mention of the man's name, the former Chief Executive visibly winced saying, "Well Mr. Grant, I wouldn't exactly say that I'm in 'Dutch' as you put it but as you well know, there was that little flap in '63 about the ship we asked him to build. He was happy as a mule in a briar patch when he finally received payment from Congress. I suppose that we are still on speaking terms. What did you have in mind?"

Grant's face lit up with a sort of sadistic grin that his wife and those closest to him knew meant that he was on the verge of some great plan. He looked at the other men in the carriage and said, "I would like to get Mr. Ericsson's assessment of who he believes to be the most capable commander in our Navy and also to see what suggestions that he might have about shoring up our defenses in that area."

At this Chamberlain nodded and said to Grant, "Sir, might I suggest that as an Infantry commander for the field, we try to get someone with experience in unorthodox warfare?"

Grant looked at he scholar-turned-war hero and said, "I assume by your suggestion that you already have someone in mind?"

Chamberlain nodded and for a moment he paused as if

he were trying to phrase his next statement just so and said, "I think that we need General Sherman back!"

At this, Grant, Lincoln and the two women turned and stared at Chamberlain as if they could not believe what they had just heard. Finally Mrs. Grant spoke up and said, "You mean the man who once said 'The only good Indian is a dead Indian'?" Don't you think that is a little bit risky given what the Six Nations have been through and the fact that the Confederacy has granted them autonomy in the New Mexico Territory since we ceded that to them as part of the Peace Treaty?"

Grant thought about this a moment and then said, "No, Julia I think that Mr. Chamberlain may be right, Sherman knows Indian tactics and ever since the war it's become pretty clear that the nature of warfare has changed. The only problem with the last war was the fact that we just didn't see that things had changed until it was too late. We failed to see that the weapons had gotten better but the tactics hadn't. It took 600,000 dead soldiers to show us how blind we commanders had been. That cannot be allowed to happen again."

Lincoln nodded and then said to Mrs. Grant, "Madam, now you realize why I chose your husband to lead the nation's armies in the late war. I only wish I would have seen it sooner, and then perhaps some of those men would not have had to die to show us where we went wrong."

Grant smiled a sad kind of knowing smile and said, "Don't be too hard on yourself sir, I'm not so sure that I would have been the man for the job in '61. I didn't have a lot of faith in my abilities then."

Lincoln nodded and then said, "Alright, that takes care of the Cavalry and the Infantry. We'll have to wait and see about the Navy. What about the Artillery?"

At this they all stared at each other as if physically searching each other for a name. After what seemed like several minutes, Grant said to them, "Let's not think on it any more tonight, we'll wait until we're back in Washington and then we can get more people in on this to help hammer out the details.

Once back in Washington, Grant, Lincoln and Chamberlain gathered in the library of the White House to discuss further military appointments. Telegrams had been sent to Sherman and Devin. Now their attention turned to finding capable field commanders for the Artillery and the Naval & Marine forces. After much discussion and a telegram to former Artillery Chief Henry Hunt, the decision was made to compile a list of possible replacements and interview them and pick the most capable applicant. The initial phase of the process, which was to compile the list, took several days. Many names were considered and many others were just as quickly discounted. Several of the names, which were discussed, were now either serving with or retired from service with the Confederate States Army. Such was the case with E.P. Alexander, H.N. Pendleton and many others.

There was even a short-lived discussion on the

possibility of recruiting either General Jackson or R.E. Lee, Jr. the former having had long experience in both commanding field artillery and also instructing the cadet classes at V.M.I. in the art of placing and properly utilizing the big guns. The latter had served during the late war in the famous (or infamous, however you chose to view it) Rockbridge Light Artillery. Both of these were rapidly discarded owing to the fact that it was felt that some of the "old-timers" in the current Army's artillery corps would take a dim view of being commanded by their old adversaries.

Finally it was decided to promote the most senior commander that they could find that had practical experience on the big guns. Their chosen man was Colonel William Randall. Randall was a graduate of West Point (class of '46) and a veteran of both the Mexican War and the War Between the States. He had served as a young Second Lieutenant along side, of all people, General (then Major) Thomas Jonathan Jackson.

Randall was a Pennsylvanian who had enlisted in the army after the fall of Fort Sumter. He had left the army after having served with the 4th Artillery in Mexico and a short tour in the desert southwest fighting the Apache and Comanche. When the War Between the States broke out, Randall had sought out Governor Curtin of Pennsylvania and had volunteered his services in any way that the Governor saw fit. Curtin immediately seized this excellent opportunity and had appointed the young officer (now a

First Lieutenant, having received a brevet for bravery at Cerro Gordo), as a recruiting officer for artillery units that were now being organized in answer to President Lincolns call for 300,000 volunteers.

It was a daunting task but the young and dashing officer was equal to the task. He rapidly organized the first 10 batteries, getting the men and equipment coordinated and the training of the neophyte gunners underway. He was often seen walking up and down the training field observing the training, greeting and encouraging the men and sometimes stepping in to instruct them personally or point out a mistake but always doing so in a way that the men felt that he truly had their best interests at heart, which of course he did.

After having organized these batteries and preparing them to fight, Randall requested a field command. He realized early on that even though he was a capable organizer and administrator, his true strength was that of a battlefield officer. After much cajoling, Governor Curtin acquiesced to Randall's request and gave him command of the 2nd Pennsylvania Volunteer Light Artillery with the accompanying promotion to Captain, as the position required.

This unit served with great distinction thanks in great degree to the pre-combat training and organization provided by the very capable young officer. He was eventually elevated to the rank of Major and awarded the Medal of Honor for valor after having stepped up and manned a position on one of the battery's 3-inch Ordnance Rifles which was in danger of falling into enemy hands when a majority of the crew was killed or wounded during one of the Seven Days' Battles.

After the war, Randall went back to Pennsylvania and tried his hand at more banal pursuits. He tried running for elected office, but was defeated. He worked as a police officer in Philadelphia but was quickly bored and resigned. He worked at numerous jobs and finally found that his administrative skills made him a valuable asset in the steel making industry.

His lucky break came when he was in Pittsburgh for a meeting of Civil War veterans and happened to meet Andrew Carnegie who talked with the young man for a great long time and, seeing something promising in the young man, offered him a job as a purchasing and disbursement agent. However, this too was too mundane a task for a man who had seen battle. After much soul searching and after a long discussion with his wife, Randall decided to put his uniform back on and do what he knew best.

When Randall received his telegram offering him a promotion to Brigadier General and naming him as the Overall Artillery Commander for the entire United States Army, he was lecturing the commanders of the various batteries that still surrounded Washington. He repeatedly challenged them to remember the conflicts of the past and to try and learn from their mistakes.

CHAPTER 9
STEAM & SAIL

There was a stiff breeze blowing through the rigging and it made the ropes vibrate with a low, almost imperceptible hum. You felt it more than heard it and it was this hum that the man checking the ratlines felt from the soles of his bare feet to the top of his head. It was the hum that had been a constant companion to him for nearly thirty years.

His name was Commander James O'Kane. His career in the Navy began at age ten when he went to sea as a cabin boy on a merchant ship. He spent the next seven years learning the art of seamanship and at age 17 applied to and gained admission to the Naval Academy at Annapolis, Maryland. He graduated in the top third of his class and at the outset of the Civil War was assigned to the position of Flag Lieutenant under Rear Admiral Dahlgren. After the war he served as Executive officer on the U.S.S. Harriet Lane patrolling the waters off the east coast of the United States.

It was this duty that gained him the reputation of being an expert seaman. The Harriet Lane was a large, heavily armed ship that had made a reputation for herself during the war that had saved the ship from almost certain doom afterwards. She had been built almost 20 years before and had seen better days, but her sheer size and the number of guns on her decks made her a formidable force. Capable of up to 12 knots under steam using the two large side wheels, she could also be rigged Brigantine fashion to conserve on coal. It was this rigging that the Commander was now checking aloft.

His men admired him because he would not ask them to do anything that he himself would not do. That was exactly what he was doing at this moment. Normally, a sailor of more common rating would be tasked with the job of checking the "rat lines". In fact, a sailor had checked them not two hours beforehand. It was Commander O'Kane's nerves that had him doing this task for no other reason than to calm down.

He had received orders to report to the Secretary of the Navy's office in Washington. The prospect of this both pleased and frightened him. He could not wait to see his old commanding officer, Admiral Dahlgren, who was now the Secretary of the Navy. On the other hand, he could not think of anything that he had done which would warrant such a summons. Many were the times he had seen men's careers end with just such a visit. He could think of no good reason why he would be called to Washington. After all this time, it did not seem to him that Admiral Dahlgren would just call him to his office out of some sense of sentimentality. No, it had to be something else, but what?

Like many of the old-timers in the Navy, O'Kane remembered a time when all ships were made of wood and the wind was your only source of power. He had seen his Navy change from sail to steam in just a few short years. He wondered, "What new development will they come up with next?"

He had seen the new "Ironclad" navy and had been astonished and a bit repulsed at the thought of cruising around the seas trapped inside what amounted to an iron wrapped canoe. He could not imagine not being able to feel the wind in his face and smell the salt air. He could never bring himself to command such a vessel.

Then the thought hit him; maybe he was being summoned to Washington in order for him to receive a promotion and possibly his own command. His time in the service and his time in his current rank more than warranted a promotion to Captain and command of his own ship.

"God." he thought, "Please don't let it be one of those infernal floating boilers!"

Little did he realize just how close to the facts of the matter he was. Yet he could never imagine just what sort of odd twists his fate and the fate of the country had in store for him.

He made the trip from Baltimore to Washington by train. He had never liked trains and had gone out of his way to avoid having to ride them. His time spent at sea was a perfect way to keep him from having to endure the noise, smoke and endless boredom of a long train ride just like this one. He thought, "If I live through this and I get a promotion and my own command, I am never riding one of these blasted things again. I'll be buried at sea first!"

After a while he began to doze off and before he could get comfortable enough to get any really meaningful sleep, he heard the conductor announce over the increasing noise of the brakes and the screeching of the wheels on the rails that they had arrived at their destination. Looking out the window near his seat, he noticed a sleek, black carriage with a matched pair of dappled grays. He thought, "Must be someone pretty important coming in today."

To his shock and amazement, as he passed the driver of the fancy rig, the man looked directly at him and said, "Commander O'Kane, come with me please. The President is waiting to see you."

O'Kane was still in shock a full hour after his arrival at the White House. While he was still trying to comprehend the words that the driver had said his bag was being hoisted into the boot of the carriage and a rail steward was holding the door to the carriage open. He felt like saying to the men, "You must be looking for someone else; all of this can't be for just me."

He allowed himself to be helped up into the plush interior of the coach. Just for a moment, he caught himself looking around and thinking to himself, "I could get used to this!"

After what seemed like only a couple of minutes—

strangely, he found himself unable to gauge time on land—the coach stopped under the portico of the White House. There a liveried doorman met him along with a man that he thought looked vaguely familiar. It was not until he had been escorted into the Oval office that he was able to identify the man as Alan Pinkerton, head of the U.S. Secret Service. Pinkerton ushered him in and quietly backed out the door and closed it behind him. There before him, facing the window with his back towards O'Kane was the man at whose leisure O'Kane served, President Ulysses S. Grant.

Grant paused a moment for effect after he heard Pinkerton exit. Slowly he turned to face the young man who had come so highly recommended by his Secretary of the Navy. What he saw before him was everything that he himself could have asked for in a prospective Chief of Naval Operations.

At nearly six feet, O'Kane was taller than the Chief Executive by several inches. He had the broad shoulders and narrow waist and hips of a man who had spent a lifetime hauling the lines on a ship. His hair was dark and wavy, a bit longer than was appropriate for an officer, Grant thought. However, what got Grant's attention were the man's eyes. They were the color of a winter's sky, sometimes blue and, when his mood changed sometimes gray. Grant could not shift his gaze from the man's eyes as he stood at attention in front of the President's desk.

After what seemed like an hour but was in reality only

minutes, the President spoke. "At ease Commander, take a seat. We have something of great importance to discuss. I have a situation that needs a man of your unique abilities and experience."

O'Kane was about to say something, more because he thought he should than the fact that he had anything of value to say when the President continued with his line of conversation. Grant looked across the wide, dark expanse that was his desk and said to O'Kane, "Let me spell this out for you Commander, the Confederacy is in bad shape. She just lost her President and they have a relative neophyte taking over. Longstreet was a capable field commander and I have no doubt that given time, he will prove himself a capable administrator of the public trust. However, it is my fear and the fear of a great many men who are much more politically astute than I, that he does not have that luxury. Clearly, the English are up to something, although at the moment we are at a loss to say what."

At that moment there was a knock at the door. Grant said, "Come". The door opened and a group of men came in. O'Kane sat in disbelief as many of the men that not only he, but the entire country came to regard as heroes in the late war walked into the Oval Office as if they were regular visitors to this inner sanctum. The names were like a religious litany of patriotism—Chamberlain, Lincoln, Dahlgren, Sherman, Devin, and Pinkerton. There were two men that he did not recognize and Secretary Dahlgren dispensed with the pleasantries and simply said, "Commander O'Kane, this is Brigadier General William Randall, Chief of Artillery, and Mr. Alfred Thomas, one of Mr. Pinkerton's operatives."

The shook hands and regained their seats. After about a minute seated around the table with many of his nations legendary leaders, O'Kane's curiosity began to get the better of him. Finally as they exchanged small talk and the odd remembrance of the war, O'Kane finally broke the mood by asking, "Mr. President, I don't want to sound rude or ungrateful for the excellent treatment that I have received since my arrival but would you mind telling me why I was summoned here in the first place? I understand the dilemma that The Confederacy finds itself in but I fail to understand what that means to the United States in general and to me in particular."

The men all looked at each other and shared a knowing smile. Dahlgren turned to his former Lieutenant and said simply, "My boy, you're here to take over as Chief of Naval Operations at sea. You have been promoted to the rank of Commodore and your name has been placed on the short list for promotion to Rear Admiral. Said promotion to take effect thirty days after the current situation stabilizes itself or, immediately upon an active declaration of hostilities."

There were nods around the table as if to punctuate the words of the Secretary and to give them added weight and veracity. O'Kane was in shock. He had come expecting a promotion and his own ship and instead he got two promotions with the promise of a third and, he had command of every naval vessel, seaman, officer and marine that was currently in his country's arsenal. O'Kane's first question was, "Who commands the Marines?" Grant looked at him and said, "Don't ask us, you're in command!"

O'Kane's mind began reeling at the prospect. Grant's words had been the validation of what O'Kane had begun to think was nothing but a dream. He decided right there and then that his first duty from that point on would be to assure that the President's and by extension, the country's trust in him would never be broken except by his death.

As his first act as the new Chief of Naval Operations (sea), O'Kane searched for and found the most capable Marine officer that he could find. Major Michael Hudson had been a Marine sergeant during the war and had seen heavy fighting on board the ram *Tennessee* during the battle in Mobile Bay. Awarded the Medal of Honor for that action, Hudson was given a field promotion to Lieutenant and from that point on he applied the same grit and determination that had allowed him to overcome great odds and win his nation's highest award.

Currently assigned as an instructor at the Naval Academy at Annapolis, Maryland, Hudson was as surprised as his new superior was when informed of his new duties. In true Marine fashion though, Hudson never let his surprise manifest itself on his stern features. A native of County Sligo Ireland, Hudson had grown up knowing that any outward sign of weakness would almost assuredly bring an attack if not physically then emotionally. It was this knowledge that had served Hudson well in the Corps. He did not consider anything that he had done in his career as remarkable. He had simply seen a job to be done and did it. It was this quality that Commodore(Rear Admiral select) O'Kane had seen in the man and realized it for what it was. O'Kane arranged to meet with Hudson and brief him in on the situation at hand as he understood it.

Commodore O'Kane went to Annapolis to meet with Major Hudson, stopping only long enough at a Washington tailor's shop to have a couple of new uniforms made. He stood in front of a full-length mirror, admiring the handiwork of the tailor and his assistant. He still could not get over the numerous, thick bands of gold braid on the sleeve of the dark blue coat. Never in his wildest dreams had he ever imagined that he would rise so far. At least when he received his next promotion, the only thing that he would have to have done to his uniforms would be to have another row of braid added.

Satisfied with the overall effect of his appearance, O'Kane traveled by train to Annapolis and arriving there, headed straight for his meeting with Hudson. The two men met in the Major's office at the Academy. It had been nearly 20 years since O'Kane had walked the corridors of the school. The memories of his cadet days flooded over him and it was almost like a dream as he found his feet leading him to Hudson's office almost on their own accord.

Major Hudson greeted his visitor with a sharp salute and promptly invited him into his office and offered him a chair. After the Commodore was seated, Hudson sat behind his desk and waited for his visitor to explain the nature of his visit. It was against military protocols for the lower ranked officer to question the motives of his superior. Hudson was not disappointed. As it turned out, O'Kane had no intention of making his subordinate wait for the information. In fact, O'Kane considered it of paramount importance to bring the Major up to speed as rapidly as possible.

"Major", O'Kane began, "What I am about to tell you does not leave this room is that understood?"

"Yes sir!" answered Hudson.

He had already figured that much out since it was clear that this was important due to the fact that they had sent such a high ranking officer to meet with him. "The President and several of his advisors think that we might be in danger of attack in the next few weeks. With the death of President Lee and the succession of Vice President Longstreet to the Presidency, it may be that there are those in Richmond that will advocate a resumption of hostilities between our two countries. It is also considered a possibility that Great Britain may attempt to capitalize on the instability in the South and attempt to re-establish control of that portion of the continent to allow a further expansion into the United States and for them to re-claim their lost colonies. It is our job to see that none of these things happen, at least not from the sea. It is my belief that with you in command of our Marine forces, we will be able to exert considerable pressure to see that nothing comes of any plans in that vein."

Hudson sat looking at the man across from him and the look on his face spoke volumes. "Sir, I am honored that you would consider me a candidate for such a position and I do not mean to sound ungrateful but, and forgive me for asking this question, do you really think that any of this could actually happen?"

O'Kane studied the Marine for a moment and said, "Major, it doesn't matter whether I think that it could happen or not. What does matter is that the President and some very smart people in Washington think that it could. Our job is to be prepared for just such a contingency and to prevent it if it does. As the overall commander of all the Marine forces in the field, you will be empowered to make any adjustments to the current situation of our Marines that you deem necessary. You are hereby promoted to the rank of Colonel with a brevet of Brigadier General to be made permanent as soon as the situation stabilizes or upon the initiation of open hostilities. Oh, and off the record, I personally think that we have more to worry about with the English than with the Confederate government. They have enough on their plate without having to start any new problems."

Hudson's head was swimming with all the possibilities that what he had just learned could stir up. He looked at his superior and, after a moment taken to collect his thoughts, he stood at attention and saluted saying, "What are my orders sir?"

O'Kane smiled a brief smile at the man since this was exactly the response that he had been expecting. Over the years, he had become a decent judge of men's character and had already come to the conclusion that he had made the right choice in selecting this man for the position of overall commander of the Marines in the field.

"Your first order Colonel, is to get yourself to a tailor and have a couple of new uniforms made with your new rank on them. Have the tailor send the bill to my office and I will personally see to it that it gets paid. Second, I want a report on the status of all active Marine units with a complete accounting of combat effectives, arms, equipment and any apparent deficiencies either in type and amount of arms and equipment or in the capabilities of the officers and non-commissioned officers appointed to command the troops. I will entertain any recommendations for promotion, demotion, discharge from the Corps or disciplinary actions that you may have at that time. I want to know as soon as possible what kind of fighting shape our Marines are in and get them ready for the fight that's coming."

Hudson nodded and simply said, "Yes sir, I'll get right on it."

With that, O'Kane turned and walked out of the man's office and left him to begin the task at hand. He then went to the Superintendents office to inform him that he would need to begin to look for a replacement for his current instructor of land-based operations. The Superintendent was shocked and a bit perturbed but considering O'Kane's rank and the letter that he held signed by the President and the Secretary of the Navy, he was smart enough not to voice his opposition to what he had just been told. Next, O'Kane went to the train station and caught the next train back to Washington to report back to Secretary Dahlgren and the President that the Naval and Marine forces were now commanded by the most capable men that could be had for the job.

CHAPTER 10
PREPARING FOR BATTLE
RICHMOND, VA
DECEMBER 1870

Longstreet looked around the table at his military leaders and his cabinet and said, "Gentlemen, we now know that the English are sending two of their best regiments and several ships of the line to try and invade Richmond and overthrow this administration and this country. Now I don't know about you but I personally have fought too hard and seen too many good men die to allow that to happen."

The assembled men looked at one another at the revelation of a foreign power sending armed troops to attempt a takeover of the government. None of them had expected this to happen. Finally, it was General Jackson who asked the question that was foremost in everyone's mind. "How did we get the information that they were coming sir?"

There were nods all around the table at the question. Longstreet looked around the table at the men assembled there, paused a moment for effect and said, "We received word from the United States Secret Service that there were preparations under way to send both the Horse Guards and the Coldstream Guards here. Their orders are to establish a base of operations from which later arrivals of troops could exploit a breakthrough and make an assault on this city with orders to capture if possible, kill if necessary any and all members of the Confederate government. That includes everyone in this room and their combined families."

This revelation started a commotion in the room that took several minutes to subside. The next man to speak was the Chief of Military Intelligence, General Pickett. "We have received no such news from our operatives in Great Britain sir."

"That is because all of your operatives have either been suborned or killed General." said Longstreet.

At this, Pickett blanched and everyone in the room could read what was on his mind, "Not again, I'm losing my command again!"

Sensing just that, Longstreet continued on to try and reassure his old friend. "The fault is not yours or your agents George. They have someone over there that is an old hand at this game and very good at it. As a matter of fact, everyone in this room knows him if not personally then by reputation. His name is William Norris, formerly Major of the Confederate States Army office of Signals now, Colonel of the Queen's own Horse Guards."

Every eye in the room was locked on the President and

every mouth was suspended open in disbelief. They all knew the stories of how it was believed by some that Norris had been killed and still others believed that he had escaped the country. Now it seemed that the latter group was being vindicated. Pickett turned to his friend and said, "This has been confirmed?"

"Yes George," the President answered. "It seems that the United States Secret Service has an edge on Norris in that he doesn't personally know their agents like he does ours. They managed to infiltrate his organization over there and are reporting back regularly. I have it on good authority that he was able to renew some old associations and convince some old friends of the merit in the English plan. Those he could not convince have all turned up dead. I am sorry George, you did the best you could but you could never have planned on something like this happening. The only thing left to do is to prepare for what's coming and to make them sorry that they ever tried."

It was Jackson who spoke next saying, "Mr. President, the Army stands ready to do whatever is necessary to defend the capital. Just give me the word and I will have 10,000 men fully armed and deployed, ready to meet the oncoming threat."

Longstreet looked at his old friend and thought, "Yes, he would do just that and be right out front leading the charge if no one were there to stop him!"

Instead he said, "Thank you General, I know that you and your troops can always be relied upon to do whatever is necessary. However, let us see just where we stand in all of the critical areas and we will then formulate a plan to use what resources we have to our best advantage."

Several of the men around the table thought to themselves, "Isn't that just like old Pete, always was a man who liked to know what pieces he had to play with before he started the game!"

They all nodded and said, "Yes sir"

One by one they began giving the President the status of their various areas of responsibility. First to report was, of course General Jackson who, as previously stated had roughly 10,000 men within an easy day's march of Richmond. There were approximately another 20,000-25,000 spread out within the confines of the new Confederacy. It would take close to two weeks to get them into the same theater of operations and Longstreet gave the order to start them moving and consolidating. Next, General Stuart gave a brief report on the status of the Cavalry. He stated, "I can field about 7,500 troopers now and another 5,000 in a week to ten days."

Longstreet said, "Make it so." Stuart turned and left the room accompanied by Jackson.

The Secretary of the Navy, former Captain of the C.S.S. Alabama, Rafael Semmes stood next and said, "Sir, we have approximately ten wooden ships of various configurations, four ironclads including the new C.S.S. Virginia with the newly modified air circulation and propulsion systems and the English Whitworth guns on board. The one thing that concerns me, sir, is that I have several able bodied seamen, masters and ensigns currently assigned to General Pickett's command as well as two companies of Marines. If we are to properly man and protect those ships, we're going to need every man we have plus we're going to have to seek out men who have experience on board ship and try and get them back."

Longstreet considered what Semmes had said and mulled it over for a moment. His mind told him to just tell Semmes to make do with what he had and not to offer too much explanation. However, something told him that the man would not just accept this blindly and so Longstreet was trapped into telling him something but at the same time maintaining some level of secrecy.

Finally he turned to Semmes and said, "Mr. Secretary, General Pickett's group is working on a project which may greatly impact what is going to happen here in the coming weeks, I cannot spare the men he has under his command at this time. You will have to find men to take their places and trust me that this is the right thing to do. I will help you all that I can in this task but the project that General Pickett is developing could be the difference between life and death for this country of ours."

Semmes knew Longstreet well enough if not from directly working under him then by reputation to know that if the man thought that something was of critical importance, then it simply was. Semmes looked at his Commander-in-Chief and simply said, "Yes sir, with your permission I will get started right away."

Longstreet nodded and silently breathed a sigh of relief at not having to explain himself further. He said to Semmes as he passed him on the way out of the room, "Thank you for understanding and not pressing the issue."

Semmes nodded and said, "Sir, I have always known you to be a capable commander and I know you would not ask such a thing if it were not absolutely necessary."

The other men in the room gave their accounting of the situations that they were facing and one by one, Longstreet assured them that he would do his best to see that most if not all of their most critical needs were met as soon as possible. The last man in the room with Longstreet was Pickett and the two men sat at a small side table and Longstreet started the conversation by asking the question, "Where do we stand with the "boats" George?"

Pickett smiled at his former commander and said, "Sir, I have three identical craft fully equipped and standing by with full crews at the secret location on the York/James peninsula."

At this revelation, Longstreet's mouth dropped open and he said, "Three? I thought that there was only one!"

Pickett shook his head and said, "As soon as we had worked all the bugs out of the design, we started construction on two more simultaneously. They were completed less than two weeks ago. Both have had their initial sea trials running up and down the rivers and I was just about to order them out to open water tonight or tomorrow night to try some maneuvers and to shake them down."

Longstreet thought about the wisdom of sending the boats out at night. There was less of a chance that anyone would accidentally see one prowling the coast. After all, the Marines couldn't exactly follow the boats and provide complete security. Longstreet knew now that what he was about to do was the right move.

"George" he said, "as you know, when the old man died, I took over as the new president. What you may or may not have noticed is that I never have selected anyone to succeed me in my job as Vice President. I had hoped to have a little more time to make a decision on that. However, events being what they are, my hand is being forced. I don't know if you realize how much I have relied on you in the past and how much I have relied on you in the past few weeks. I value our friendship and I value your abilities and your keen analytical mind. It is for that reason that I would very much like you to consider carefully what I am about to ask you. George, I want you to step down from your position as Chief of Military Intelligence and be my Vice President."

The look on Pickett's face was priceless. For once, someone had said something so totally shocking that the man had no ready answer. Longstreet chuckled inwardly and thought, "Finally gave you something that you couldn't turn into some big joke didn't I?

After a few moments, Pickett regained his composure

and said, "Sir you honor me with your offer. I will serve this country in whatever capacity I can and I will do so to the best of my ability."

"I know you will George, and your first order of business is to name a new Chief of Military Intelligence and make any adjustments to the current 'Project' as you see fit before you go."

Pickett smiled one of his trademark impish grins and said to his superior, "I'm already one step ahead of you on that one sir, I would like your permission to appoint Major Dixon as overall commander of our new 'Submarine and Torpedo Service' with a promotion to Lieutenant Colonel."

Longstreet nodded. Pickett continued with the next part of his plan without waiting to be asked to continue. He said, "Sir, I know that there are several men who are quite capable of taking over the office of Chief of Military Intelligence but there is a young man that I have been keeping my eye on and to put it mildly, the boy's a genius. He comes up with ideas that I can't even follow. He catches on to things as naturally as you and I take to breathing. His last posting was with me as a technical advisor on the mechanical engineering of the boats. He will take to the new job like a duck takes to water!"

Longstreet put his hands up in front of him as if fending of a blow saying, "Alright George, whatever you want to do is fine with me. Just please curb some of that enthusiasm before someone gets hurt...like me!"

Pickett feigned the demeanor of a scolded child and said

sheepishly, "Yes sir, I am sorry for endangering the President's life so!"

At this both men chuckled. Just as Pickett was about to take his leave of the President, the doors to the conference room burst open and in rushed John Bell Hood and Robert E. Lee, Jr. Both men walked to a spot a few paces from the President and saluted. Hood spoke for both men saying, "Mr. President, we are volunteering to serve the Confederacy in whatever manner you see fit to assign us."

Longstreet smiled at the two men and said, "I was wondering what kept you away THIS long! Of course we can use you. General Hood, you are hereby restored to active duty and your first order of business is to get yourself to a tailor and have yourself a couple of uniforms made to the current specifications and the increased measurements necessary to cover your frame. I daresay that civilian life has left its mark on you, in several places by the look of things!"

He chuckled at the shocked reaction of the big Texan who, it seems still had not gotten used to being the target of Longstreet's well aimed jabs, even though he had been their recipient since the pair were cadets at the Point. Next, Longstreet turned to Lee and said, "Well sir, since your employer has just enlisted his services, I suppose that it would be altogether fitting that you would want to do the same. I would ask that on only two conditions will I consider your request. First, that your mother is provided for and has all the care and comfort that she needs. Second, that you honor me, this country and the memory of your father by accepting the position of overall Artillery commander of the Confederate States Army which will carry the rank of Major General."

The young man looked in shock at his new Commander-in-Chief and said, "Sir, I never held rank above that of a Captain. How will this sit with the older more experienced artillery officers in the service?"

Longstreet regarded the question and looked at the young man and after a few seconds he answered saying, "Son, I don't think that there is a man in this army that would begrudge you both the position and the rank. We all know that you can do the job and we need a man who has experience but who also is young enough to take the field and show some initiative."

Lee regarded the President for a moment and finally said, "Sir, I accept your most generous offer. What are my orders?"

Longstreet smiled and said, "First, go with General Hood and get fitted for a uniform. Second, take stock of what we have in the way of artillery and then submit a report to me with your recommendations as regarding officers; who's fit, who's unfit, etc. I want to know how many guns, what kind and what is the status of our ordnance. Make me a wish list of the things that you think we will need to make this work."

Lee snapped to attention and saluted saying, "Yes sir, you will have the report by 8:00 AM tomorrow."

This surprised Longstreet since it was well past 5:00 PM now. Lee would be up half the night gathering the information needed to file his report. Longstreet looked at the three men gathered around him and said, "Gentlemen, you have your orders, carry them out. Dismissed."

The men all saluted, turned and left the President's office in pursuit of their individual missions. The next day when they came to deliver their individual reports, Longstreet was delighted to see that Hood and Lee had both indeed been to the tailor's shop and that both men now wore uniforms of the type currently described in the Confederate Army's Regulation manual. The sole point on which Longstreet could find fault was that the coat worn by General Lee sported only the rank insignia of a Colonel.

When questioned as to why he did not have his proper rank displayed, Lee simply said, "I did not think it proper to wear a rank that is so far above my previous one. I chose instead to wear the rank of a Colonel due to the post in which I am engaged and also because if it was good enough for my father, then it is good enough for me!"

Longstreet smiled at the young man and said, "General, I will respect your judgment in this matter and tell you that despite what you may think of your previous experience, your expertise in the artillery will be of invaluable service to this country. I will only say that you are truly your father's son and that I expected nothing less than this. Your father thought that it would be considered by some as prideful if he wore the rank that had been bestowed on him. He never aspired to be anything more than a good soldier. I can see now that this is the legacy that he has left to you. If you are half the soldier that I think you are, this country could not find a better man for the job!"

Lee's cheeks colored at the compliment paid to him by Longstreet. To play off the situation, Lee made his report verbally, which was exactly what he had written out on the sheets of paper Longstreet now held in his hands. Longstreet saw that the oral report was verbatim so he did not worry about missing anything as it was there in his hands to refer back to if he had any questions. Overall, the reports from his commanders were good in that the President found himself in better shape than he expected. "Leave it to the General to have things up to speed," he thought.

He found that besides the troops that were currently out of his control, He generally had everything that he needed to carry the battle to the enemy. He made notes on a pad of paper concerning those things that his commanders wanted or needed.

"I'll put George to work on this once I know where we stand." he thought.

He knew that Pickett had a great talent for procuring, organizing and supplying the men in the field with whatever they needed. It was at that moment when the unexpected happened. A courier came in carrying a piece of paper, which Longstreet recognized as a sheet from one of the telegraph operator's pads that were the communications medium currently in use. The courier handed the message to Longstreet without speaking and as quickly as he came, he turned and strode off in the direction that he had come. Longstreet opened the piece of folded paper and quickly read the brief message it contained. After allowing what he had just read to sink in, he whistled a low note that signified that he had just received a bit of unwelcome news.

"Gentlemen" Longstreet said. "I have just received word from our friends to the North that the British have dispatched four of their largest warships with a half dozen more to follow as they are outfitted, loaded and made ready for sea travel. I also have the assurances of President Grant that the United States Navy stands ready to intercept those vessels and turn them back in the direction that they came. If they are fired upon in this action, then they will return fire and then they will join forces with our Army and Navy to turn away any foreign military forces that attempt to make landfall either in the Confederacy or in the United States."

Eyebrows shot up all around the room and Secretaries and Staff Officers sent their subordinates scurrying to make last minute preparations and deployments. It was one of these subordinates that left and came back a few moments later accompanied by two soldiers carrying a large stand on which had been placed a map of the eastern coast of both the United States and the Confederate States. As soon as the map was in place and secure, junior officers began using grease pencils, rulers and other instruments to show the deployment of ships and men as well as the progress of the British invasion fleet. As near as they could tell, they had just about two weeks before they had to face the two crack regiments being arrayed against them. That was not much time especially considering what was left to be done.

At the mention of this, Longstreet called to a member of his staff and said, "Have the carriage brought around and have my bags packed for a trip to Washington, D.C. I need to talk to President Grant face to face.

The assembled men looked at each other and shook their heads as if to say, "What could possibly go wrong next?"

Longstreet recognized these looks for what they were and said, "Relax gentlemen, it seems that my counterpart in the United States has been watching the situation with great interest and now wishes to lend whatever assistance we may need in the coming conflict."

At this many of the faces changed expressions from worry to astonishment. Could it be that after three bloody years of war and seven years of an uneasy peace the two countries had truly separated to the point where relations could now begin to normalize? Many in the room did not believe it could be so. They would soon find out how far their former enemy would go to actually ensure the survival of the new nation.

CHAPTER 11

ALLIANCES

NEAR WASHINGTON, D.C.
NOVEMBER 20, 1870

"Thank you for meeting with me on such short notice Mr. President." Longstreet said.

"When I received your telegraph message that you wanted to meet with me about the British invasion force heading for Richmond, I knew it was time that we put our heads together and came up with a plan to give them a warm reception." Grant replied.

The two men were meeting in the same tobacco barn that John Wilkes Booth and his co-conspirators had planned to use as a rendezvous point following the failed assassination attempt on then-President Lincoln over five years previous. Both of the men commented on the irony of the location for their meeting given the fact that it had been a British-influenced plot in the first place.

Both men knew that a chance passerby would not disturb them since both men had been accompanied by a three-man security detail, which they had agreed upon in their communiqués to each other. The six men were arrayed around the building, carefully concealed in the woods surrounding the structure. The three men of President Grant's detail had all been sharpshooters during the War Between the States. Two had served in the now famous 1st and 2nd U.S. Sharpshooters Regiments more familiarly known by the sobriquet "Berdan's Sharpshooters" so named for their commanding officer Colonel Hiram Berdan, who was himself an expert with a rifle. The third had served with the 42nd Pennsylvania Volunteers, alternately known as "Kane's Rifles" or "The Bucktails". All had been part of some of the fiercest fighting of the war. President Longstreet was accompanied by three former members of General William

Barksdale's Mississippi Sharpshooters. It was that group of men who had given General Ambrose Burnside's troops something to worry about as they attempted to build their pontoon bridges across the Rappahannock River outside the city of Fredericksburg. As the six men maintained their vigil outside the barn, inside the two Chiefs-of-State went over their lists of assets and liabilities. Grant said, "I have six iron clad ships and over a dozen more wooden-hulled frigates and other similarly rigged ships of the line. All are heavily armed with the most up-to-date rifled pieces available in the world. Many of them are breechloaders which are twice as fast to load and fire as the old muzzle loading kind."

Longstreet nodded at this and said, "Very good sir, we can add our own four such ships to the count. Although,

I daresay that yours are probably a good bit better constructed and from what you have told me, much better armed than our ships but never fear, we shall show those rascals what can be accomplished with Southern guts and Southern iron!"

Grant chuckled at the Confederate President's uncharacteristic show of emotion and said, "You forget sir that I am all too familiar with what can be done with Southern guts and Southern iron. Almost makes me feel sorry for the Brits...almost!

At that Longstreet let out a belly laugh that took Grant by surprise and, even though he would never admit it, at least to anyone but himself it made Longstreet feel good for a change. The one thing that troubled Longstreet was just what information he should share with Grant. As a soldier, he knew about the importance of knowing exactly what his assets were and how best to use them. On the other hand, the politician in him knew of the need to maintain a certain level of secrecy in order to gain or maintain the advantage against a possible adversary. It was this conundrum that held Longstreet deep in thought until he at last realized that Grant was speaking to him in a somewhat irritated manner saying, "Mr. President, I realize that you are as concerned for the welfare of your country as I am for mine but I hardly think that this is the time for daydreaming!"

Longstreet looked at the man, his piercing gaze and the ever-present look of determination and suddenly decided,

"I must tell him about the 'boats'. It is only fair that he knows what we have as a hold card."

With that thought he turned to face his counterpart and said, " I am sorry Mr. President if I seem a bit pre-occupied but there is something that you need to know about which we have been working on since before my taking the office of President of the Confederacy."

Grant's eyebrows arched in a questioning manner and he said, "This wouldn't have anything to do with all the increased activity at the Tredegar Iron works a few years back would it?"

Now it was Longstreet's turn to show surprise. "You knew about that and yet you did nothing to stop it?" he asked.

"Didn't know if we had anything to worry about so we just let you be," Grant said. "We even thought that it might be in our best interest to let you go about the task of re-building your military. Just in case something like this was ever to happen, you understand."

At this Longstreet smiled and said, "Mr. President, what I am about to tell you will probably shock you and cause you to reevaluate your decision but I promise you that once I have finished explaining, you will quickly see just what kind of a real advantage we now have."

Grant settled back on the crate on which he had been sitting and said, "Go on."

With that, Longstreet proceeded to tell him about the secret base on the James River. An hour later, a stunned

U.S. Grant sat in disbelief across from his Confederate counterpart. For several minutes he sat, staring into space like a man in a trance and just as Longstreet was about to check for signs of life, Grant turned his head, a strange light in his eyes and the trademark boyish grin on his face that warned all who had ever seen it, that a plan was in the making.

"Pete", he said, for the first time allowing himself to use the nickname that he himself had given to Longstreet all those years ago when they were wet nosed cadets on the Hudson, "I think that we have a unique opportunity that has just been handed to us and I think that we would be foolish not to use it."

Longstreet looked at his old friend and, feeling the old camaraderie coming back to him said, "Yes Sam I think you're right. Now what are we going to do about it?"

Grant beamed a broad grin and simply said, "We're gonna whup 'em!"

Grant and Longstreet spent the next two hours going over Grant's preliminary plan and Longstreet was surprised to see that Grant's genius for tactics had somehow miraculously transferred itself to an understanding of naval tactics as well. Grant explained this by saying, "It's really not that much different from infantry or cavalry when you think of a ship in terms of a regiment and a fleet of ships in terms of a division or a corps."

Longstreet nodded his understanding of his friend's

analogy. If you thought of it in those terms, individual ship movements and movements of large numbers of ships were as easily planned for and carried out as moving a company of men from column of fours into line of battle. Grant's plan was a simple one and Longstreet was easily convinced of its merits but he suggested that rather than fall into the same trap as the generals that had dreamed up so many of the grandiose and tragically flawed campaigns and battles in the late war, that they should leave the details to the men who sailed the ships. Grant agreed and they made arrangements for Commodore O'Kane and the man selected by Confederate Secretary of the Navy Semmes to lead his nation's navy into battle. A man who, like O'Kane had risen from the ranks in relative obscurity. He was considered his navy's rising star. His name was Lieutenant Commander James Iredell Waddell. Born in Pittsboro, N.C. he had served during the Mexican War at the blockade of Vera Cruz. Being a Southerner by birth, Waddell's sympathies lay with the south at the outbreak of hostilities in 1861. He resigned his commission in the Federal navy and secretly traveled south to enlist in that country's navy. Due to the lack of ships, Waddell served in the Confederate artillery in such high profile battles as New Orleans, Louisiana, Drewery's Bluff, Virginia and Charleston, S.C.

In the seven years since the end of the war he had served on both ships of the line and in administrative posts showed himself to be capable under any condition.

It was this ability to adapt to the task at hand which had first caught the attention of Secretary Semmes. It was only after many weeks of extolling the young man's virtues that the Secretary finally convinced President Longstreet to acquiesce to the appointment of Waddell as the overall Commander (at sea) of the Confederate States Navy. The assignment was not without its positive aspects. As a result of his new posting, Waddell received a promotion to Commodore from President Longstreet himself with Secretary Semmes in attendance. It was at this meeting that the President and Secretary of the Navy informed Waddell of his first order of business once he had secured the proper uniform for his newly acquired rank. Waddell met with O'Kane on three separate occasions in much the same manner as their respective Chief Executives had some two weeks ago.

The results of their meetings were nothing short of spectacular. Their plan was to use their wooden and some of the ironclad surface ships to interdict the incoming British troop ships and to inflict as much damage as possible while keeping the transports well out to sea. A second tier of surface ships supported by the Confederate 'submerged boats' as they were now being called by those who knew of their existence, would intercept and capture or sink anything that got past the first tier of blockading ships. This was an especially ironic time for the Confederate government and those old enough to remember the hardships caused by the Federal blockade of the Southern ports. The only consolation now was that the ships on blockade duty were not trying to keep war materiel out of the Confederacy (except that which was being transported by the British) but to create a barrier of protection for the Confederacy's borders. Still many could not get used to the sight of wooden ships and ironclads flying the new Stars and Bars of the Confederacy sailing next to and sometimes tied alongside ships flying the recently modified 23-star U.S. flag.

CHAPTER 12

INVASION

SOMEWHERE IN THE NORTH ATLANTIC
DECEMBER 17, 1870

The four men stood on the pitching deck of the ship looking at the horizon. Each man was lost in his own thoughts. Some doubted the chances of success of their new endeavor but all had been around long enough to know the hazards of voicing such an opinion, especially with someone so nearby that obviously had the Queens ear. Each man regarded the others in surreptitious, sideways glances. All knew the risk that they were taking and the great rewards of success as well as the price of failure.

The questions on their minds were the same, "What is waiting for us? Do they suspect anything? What can we expect to find in the way of resistance?" They were all confident of the capabilities of the soldiers; sailors and marines that were on board the four large troop ships as well as the quality and quantity of the equipment and materiel on the numerous support and supply ships that accompanied them. The one thing that they could not be sure of was the intelligence report that they had received just before setting sail. They had it on the authority of one of their top operatives that neither the Confederates nor the Americans had any inkling of what was about to happen in a few short days. Their best guess was that their departure, even with the number of ships involved had gone largely unheeded. This gave many of the men assembled the sense of security that many of them needed to settle their nerves. Had they but known that their departure had been not only noted but also reported by no fewer than six operatives of the United States Secret Service, their comfort level would have immediately plummeted.

"This will be a glorious victory for Her Majesty", Fremantle said. The other two Englishmen nodded their agreement to the statement.

Only the expatriate Confederate Norris, now a colonel in the Queen's own Horse Guards, refused to share in the jubilant atmosphere taking place onboard the HMS Repulse. He turned to the others and said, "I wouldn't be so sure of myself Colonel Fremantle. For all we know, Longstreet has the whole Confederate army arrayed against us, just waiting for us to come ashore on the banks of the Chesapeake bay and starting a gigantic turkey shoot with all your boys in their fine, bright red jackets."

Norris was known for his outspoken views against the uniform of the British Army noting that regardless of the centuries old tradition that the famous "redcoat" held, in open fields, the coat was little more than an aiming stake for every enemy soldier with a rifle.

"Now see here Colonel Norris, the red coat of the British Regulars has been instilling fear in the hearts of Her Majesty's enemies for over three hundred years. I see no reason why that should not continue for this campaign. We have over two thousand crack infantrymen, three hundred heavy cannon and six hundred of the finest cavalrymen and mounts that can be found anywhere in the world." This was from Colonel Bryce Campbell, the Scottish-born commander of the Coldstream Guard, the other of the two crack regiments alluded to by Fremantle.

"Now don't get me wrong Colonel" Norris said, quickly going on the defensive with the Scotsman. "All I am saying that all of the fine uniforms and bright, shiny equipment won't do you a bit of good if you go waltzing into one of 'Old Pete's' ambushes."

Norris knew that in the years Longstreet had spent serving under Lee in the Civil War, he had learned strategy from a man who was a master at the game. He also knew that Longstreet had learned about going for the long odds when he was outnumbered and had his back against the wall. He could not explain the feeling that he had but he knew it was not good. He sensed that there was trouble ahead for the expedition in general and danger ahead for him personally. He tried to shake it off but the sensation kept bothering him well into the night and for several days thereafter. He would face whatever lie ahead and take whatever trouble came his way. This would surely spell either great wealth or great ruin for all of them. He simply turned to his companions and said simply, "Good evening gentlemen, I have a great deal to prepare for so, if you will excuse me, I will retire now to my cabin."

Each of the other men nodded and shook Norris' hand when he passed them on his way to his cabin below decks. As he was descending the ladder into the companionway on his walk back to his room, he thought, "Fools! They are committing the same error that we in the Confederacy committed years ago. They are not allowing enough flexibility in their plan to be able to change it depending on the situation."

He had seen it too many times to count. The men were marched straight into the teeth of the guns, because their officers did not have the sense to question whether the original plan now fit the circumstances. "They're going to have a bloodbath on their hands and I want to either prevent it or stop it before it takes too large of a toll on our resources." With that thought reverberating in his head, Norris went below decks to work on his plan to save the British Army from itself.

As Colonel Norris disappeared below decks, the remaining three men looked at each other and one of them said, "The man has finally let go of his senses. He honestly thinks that his former countrymen could ever stand up to the might of the British Empire and last more than a day or two."

Nods were exchanged all around along with other verbal jabs and predictions on the longevity of the Confederacy. Little did anyone realize that they were not going up solely against the Confederate forces that Longstreet had managed to marshal to deal with the invading British threat. It would soon become apparent just how badly mistaken they had been in their planning. Moreover, the results would be nothing short of disastrous.

Admiral Sir James Allerton, overall commander on sea of the invasion force, was having a word with the captain of Repulse when Fremantle and Campbell came into the cabin, which served as the wardroom of the ship. He could see that the two men were having a rather animated discussion and he did not have to guess too hard at the subject.

"Colonel Fremantle, I think that your assessment of our opponents is far too cavalier. They could very well have gotten better making war than what you observed seven years ago!" Campbell observed.

"I highly doubt that, sir. They seemed too content fighting amongst themselves to take the science of war too seriously!" Fremantle replied.

Campbell walked toward the admiral and the captain shaking his head. When he got out of earshot of Fremantle he said to the two men standing there, "And he thinks

Norris is living in a dream world! Why the man cannot even accept the possibility that the Confederates have the ability to mount any type of a serious defense. That is very dangerous thinking gentlemen."

Both men nodded their agreement with Campbell's assessment of the situation. Allerton turned to him and said, "I believe you are correct Colonel but as the Queen's personal representative to this expedition, you would be hard put to gain any concessions on that point from anyone at court, especially Her Royal Highness."

Campbell shook his head in disgust because he knew Allerton was right. "Gentlemen, I will tell you now that I do not think that we will prevail in this endeavor. We have the men and equipment necessary to complete the job but we lack leaders with the proper foresight to make the most efficient use of those elements. I would only ask one favor of you. If this goes badly and I do not survive, please be sure that the Queen knows of my reservations in this matter."

Both men promised that they would do all in their power to assure that proper notice was given to this. With that the men went their separate ways to prepare as best they could for the coming days events.

Four days later, a lookout spotted what he believed were sails on the horizon. The British officers, particularly Captain Smythe and Admiral Allerton, were surprised that there would be Confederate Navy ships patrolling this far out to sea. After a brief conference with Fremantle,

Norris and Campbell, it was determined that there was little to be done and that they would have to try and avoid being seen for as long as possible. The Admiral and the Captain conferred and a course change was ordered for the fleet. They hoped that the course correction would take them out of sight of the patrolling vessels and that they had made the correction in time. They wanted to maintain the element of surprise for as long as possible. They could not have known that the change in course would not help them maintain the secrecy of their mission but was bearing them ever closer to destiny with every league the ships traveled toward the coast.

Three hundred miles to the South and East of the British position lay part of the outer screen of ships that the two naval officers had devised when it was learned that an invasion was in the works. Part of that screen were older wooden-hulled warships while others were the more modern ironclad ships. The plan was for the larger wooden ships to engage the invading fleet and draw their fire while the smaller, more maneuverable ironclads stood in close and battered the hulls of the mostly wooden English ships. It just so happened that Commodore O'Kane's flagship, Harriet Lane, was part of the blockading force that the English fleet was closing in on at that very moment. O'Kane watched the flurry of activity around him as preparations for a naval battle of epic proportions were being made. Sailors were aloft checking sails and rigging, still others were lashing barrels and crates and bales of straw along the railing to provide the Marines with a small measure of cover from possible enemy rifle fire coming from the other ships and also from shell fragments & shrapnel from the enemy's big guns. As for the cannon on board the Harriet Lane, the gun crews were below decks checking every minute detail of each of her guns.

Stores of powder were brought up from the magazines located on the next deck down from the gun deck. Stands of shot and shell were placed so as to make them readily available to the gunners who would need them in just a few hours. Decks were scrubbed and fresh sawdust laid down. The purpose of this was to provide the gunners with a secure footing once the battle began and men began to fall. The sawdust would absorb the blood so as not to make the deck slick and difficult to stand or move around on. Every man watched the men doing this with an intensity that belied their true feelings. No one wanted to have it show on his face that he felt the least amount of fear even though to a man, they all felt it.

With preparations for battle complete, swords, cutlasses, knives, boarding axes and pikes were sharpened and guns loaded and stacked, all that was left was to wait. They didn't have long to let their fears get the worst of them. In just over an hour, lookouts spotted the sails of the invasion force coming over the horizon. A count was made of the number of ships and O'Kane knew that he did not have sufficient numbers to defeat them all on his own. His only solace was that he knew the position of every ship that the two countries had arrayed against the oncoming English invaders. His plan was a simple one; engage the enemy by taking the fight to them, inflicting as much damage on them and then turning tail and running away.

The hope was that when he turned his ships and headed for the coast, the English would believe that they had prevailed. In fact what they were doing was falling into an elaborate trap. The trap was the second echelon of ships, this time more of the small, fast ironclads and, unbeknownst to even O'Kane, six of the Confederacy's secret underwater boats. Two of these had been completed just a week before, crews working round the clock, sometimes by torchlight to complete them. Each of the boats was fitted with a forced air system through the snorkel and two torpedoes, which were deployed by means of the spar at the bow of the boat.

The only disadvantage to this was that the boat would have to put into shore or tie up beside a surface ship to allow the crew to bring the second torpedo up from its storage compartment inside the boat and then rig it to the spar for another run at the enemy's ships. The crews of the boats were less than thrilled at the thought of having to transport a live torpedo inside the boat as one might imagine. The only thing that calmed their fears was when someone pointed out that the torpedoes could be transported un-fused for safety and that the fuse could be inserted by the crew when they attached the explosive charge to the spar.

With everything done that could be done to prepare the second rank of defending ships to meet the oncoming foe, all anyone could do was wait and as anyone could tell you, that was the hardest part of all. Every ship save the underwater boats had lookouts topside scanning the horizon for any sign of a sail or evidence of a battle. They didn't have long to wait as on the third day after the initial sighting of the British force was made, Commodore O'Kane's force of blockading ships engaged the English warships just two hundred miles off the coast of the Confederacy. Fifty miles to his rear, the second echelon of ships saw, and in some cases heard, the opening shots of the Confederacy's latest fight for survival. All hoped that it would not end badly.

CHAPTER 13
Taking a Stand

O'Kane waited until the English ship was within four hundred yards before he ordered the United States' Naval ensign to be hoisted up the main mast thinking that the British might be reluctant to fire on a U.S. ship and provoke a supposed neutral country. It would not take the British long to figure out that the U.S.S. HARRIET LANE was no innocent bystander. As soon as they passed close by the British ship on her port side, O'Kane ordered the first volley from the starboard side guns. The effect was both astonishing and at the same time horrific to behold. The ship, a supply brig, was most likely carrying large amounts of gunpowder or artillery rounds because when the volley struck her side, the result was an immediate and total detonation of the entire ship. It lifted clear of the water and simultaneously vaporized along with all hands. Several of the men working the HARRIET Lane's guns stared in stunned silence while others offered up whispered prayers both for the men aboard the British ship and for their souls as well.

On board the REPULSE, Admiral Allerton swore as he

watched what was left of the HAKE, the supply ship that had just been destroyed, settle back onto the water. He knew without consulting any of the lookouts, that there would be no need to search for survivors. The HAKE carried a crew of seventy five officers and men. They were all lost along with the stores of artillery rounds that she carried. Allerton turned to the captain and ordered him to close on the ship that had just fired on his fleet. The captain gave the orders to the helmsman and at the same time, shouted orders to the signalmen on the wings of the bridge to send a message to the other ships in the fleet to disburse and to prepare to defend themselves. He hoped that the troop transports would be able to slip by without any difficulty. He was rewarded by the sight that the first of the four ships went through the blockading ships without losing more than a little of their rigging and some torn sail.

He continued to watch the other troop ships until it was clear that they were going to escape with relative ease. He gave the orders to have all ships make a run for the coast and that they would meet in a few days at a given point on the map. All of the remaining ships signaled their receipt of the message and Allerton was rewarded by the sight of the remaining ships moving away from one another and at the same time, continuing to move toward the coast.

His warships began trading shots with the combined American and Confederate vessels. The fact that he was facing the combined navies of two nations instead of one concerned Allerton to some extent but he remained confident that they would still prevail. It was during this latest assessment that the captain and the other commanders joined him on the bridge to see what could be done to extricate them from this problem. The shells were whistling above his head and every now and then, he would hear the distinct whine of a musket ball passing by.

"You seem to have found yourself a warm spot Admiral." Norris dryly observed.

"We shall see colonel" was the extent of Allerton's response to the thinly veiled barb by the former Confederate.

Norris snorted in derision at the obvious lack of concern on the part of the British flag officer. "He just doesn't get it, they have something up their sleeve and this idiot can't get it through his thick head that this is just the first round!" thought Norris.

Norris turned to Fremantle and Campbell and said, "Gentlemen, if I were you, I would make arrangements to take a smaller ship to shore and be there to rally the troops when they start landing."

The two officers looked at one another and nodded in silent agreement. The former Confederate had his faults but as a rule, stupidity was not one of them. Fremantle called to one of the signalmen and had him hail a nearby supply ship, this one a merchantman carrying stores of food and medical supplies. Them came along side to take the three officers aboard for the run to the coast.

The trip to the Virginia coast aboard the merchantman called ABIGAIL was reasonably uneventful once the captain was able to egress the area without drawing too much attention to himself. It was apparently the aim of the combined U.S. and Confederate fleets to harry the warships and troop transports but not to be too concerned with the supply ships. The three officers agreed that what happened to the HAKE was little more than a terrible case of coincidence. They were just settling down for the last leg of the journey to the coast when they saw one of their escort ships, a frigate called LANCASHIRE, lose a large section of her hull for no apparent reason. They had no way of knowing that they had just witnessed the first sinking of a naval vessel by a submerged vessel soon to be universally known as the 'submarine'.

This particular submerged vessel was the C.S.S. R.E. LEE, one of the last two HUNLEY type boats built at the secret Confederate base located on the James River peninsula. Her captain was a 26 year-old Louisiana native named James M. Morgan. Morgan had resigned as a midshipman from the Naval Academy at Annapolis at the outset of the War Between the States and had gone home hoping to secure a position in the fledgling Confederate States Navy. Unfortunately for Morgan, a lad of small stature, there did not seem to be much serious interest in him until he managed to catch the eye of one of the South's admirals and secured himself a place on board the C.S.S. McRae which served with distinction at Island #10.

After the war, Morgan, like so many other veterans tried his hand at several ventures away from the military and the sea that he loved. None of them gave him the satisfaction that he so desperately needed. So, hat in hand he went to former Confederate Secretary of the Navy Stephen Mallory to see if something could be done to get him back aboard a ship. After Mallory consulted with several members of the Lee administration, A suggestion was made that would make the best use of Morgan's small stature and his phenomenal talent for command. Morgan met with Mallory and then Chief of Military Intelligence Pickett where the latter offered Morgan a position in the Confederacy's new top-secret Submerged Boat Service.

At first Morgan met the offer with no small amount of dubious disbelief. The concept of a ship which would spend a majority of her time under water and would attack through the use of a torpedo was something that Morgan could not quite fathom yet, when he traveled to the base on the York-James Peninsula and saw the crafts for himself, his disbelief and trepidation left him immediately. Now, nearly two years later he had just become the first captain to pilot a ship under the water and to successfully plant and detonate a torpedo and sink an enemy ship. Now the R.E.LEE was tied up between two ironclads and was in the process of re-arming the spar on the front of the ship. It was Captain Morgan's intention to run back to the gun line established by the blockading fleet and wait for another target of opportunity to show itself.

Meanwhile, back on board the HARRIET LANE, O'Kane was directing the battle that was raging there. He was pacing from one corner of the quarterdeck to the other till someone made the observation that he was sure to wear a hole in the deck. The HARRIET LANE was coming to bear on a British man-of-war and O'Kane began shouting orders to the sailors and marines that scurried about her decks. The British ship came to within five hundred yards and at that distance the cannon on both ships opened fire, belching black smoke and flame but doing little to influence the tide of battle.

It wasn't the shot and shells that worried O'Kane. He was calmly watching the gun crews servicing their pieces, calmly loading, firing, cleaning and re-loading with terrible rapidity and telling accuracy. What he had not noticed was that there were Royal Marines who had taken to the rigging to use the height as an advantage to fire down into the gun crews and the men sailing the ship. O'Kane got his first indication that there was something else to fear on the British ships a moment later when several musket balls screamed past his head and buried themselves in the deck and bulkhead surrounding the U.S. Navy commander.

Just as the last of these had thudded into the deck near his feet, O'Kane heard and felt a large noise behind and to his left. Realizing it for what it was, a rifle shot, O'Kane turned just in time to see a young Marine, kneeling behind him. The Marine still held the rifle in the firing position and was concentrating on the sights. He addressed the young man saying, "That was an excellent shot Marine! What is your name?"

The young Marine private stood, turned and faced O'Kane and said, "Hathcock sir, Private Hathcock."

O'Kane smiled slightly at the young man's practiced reply and said, "Not anymore it isn't son, from now on it's Sergeant Hathcock and if you continue to shoot that way, I foresee a long career in the Marine Corps for you!"

The young Marine smiled and said, "Yes Sir, thank you, Sir." Then he turned and concentrated on clearing the Royal Marines from the rigging of any ship foolish enough to come within range of his rifle.

While O'Kane, Morgan and Hathcock had their hands full dealing with the British warships, Fremantle, Campbell and Norris used the confusion of battle to rejoin their men on the troop ships. Now, they were well clear of the fight and heading for the Virginia coast with the intention of setting up a beachhead and beginning a push toward Richmond to capture the Confederate government. They made their way into the harbor at Newport News and began lowering the whaleboats in preparation to ferry troops ashore. There was no resistance, so the three commanders congratulated themselves on achieving complete surprise. What they did not know was that at that moment, they were being observed by a group of men just over a quarter of a mile away. Had they wanted to, the men could have unleashed an artillery barrage that, while not totally destroying the enemy, would have severely handicapped his efforts to establish the beachhead he so greatly desired.

However, the men did not fire on the British troops. Their mission was one of surveillance and intelligence gathering. After all, *Major* Norris had trained them well. So well, that they were now, almost to a man, obsessed with paying back their former leader for the treachery that had befallen their comrades and had cost so many lives. After nearly an hour of observing the landing, the ten man detail mounted their horses and rode quietly but quickly away. Their horses' hooves were bound in rags so as to prevent any noise as were all buckles and other metal parts of their bridles, saddles, guns and personal equipment. Silently as wraiths they departed the area to take the information of what they had seen to President Longstreet and the other military commanders who would then decide where their best chance for an ambush would be.

They rode several miles in total silence before they stopped to check their back trail for anyone following and then they held a brief council of war to determine what to do next. After a few moments, it was clear that they had not been followed and that they could now converse without fear of detection. The agent in charge gathered the others around him and said, "Well boys, it looks like the Yankee information checks out. Norris has thrown his hat into the ring with the redcoats!"

"Well, we'll make sure that he regrets that decision, won't we boys?" said another.

There were nods all through the group. All had had friends bribed away or killed as a direct result of Norris' treachery. Each man secretly hoped that he would be the one to catch Norris and that they would have an opportunity to get the man alone where they could visit some measure of retribution on him.

Once back at the farmhouse that now served as the headquarters for the joint C.S./U.S. force that had been assembled to meet and beat back the invaders, the leader of the group, a captain who had once ridden with Nathan Bedford Forrest, reported what the group had observed from their position. Sherman and the other U.S. officers sat around a large table that had once served as a tobacco cutting table. There with them were Hood, Lee and Stuart representing the Confederate Army's infantry, artillery and cavalry arms. The assembly of officers listened in stunned silence as the man before them gave his report.

"Sirs, my men and I observed two full regiments; that is two thousand men, their accompanying officers and the various pieces of materiel that would be needed to supply and support a detachment of that size for any length of time in the field. They had blacksmiths, farriers, artificers, coopers, wheelwrights and any other trade you can imagine. They had about a thousand pieces of artillery of every description that you can imagine, Whitworths, Napoleons, Mortars even a few of those new rapid-fire guns from Mr. Gatling that are capable of over 100 rounds a minute. In my opinion gentlemen, they are here and they have no intention of leaving unless we make them."

The officers looked at each other and then at the man who had delivered the bleak report that they had all just heard. As they talked amongst themselves, a man entered the building. After presenting himself to the officers, he began to tell them about an idea that he had that would allow the forces gathered to meet this invasion to not only hold it back, but would also allow the combined U.S./C.S. force to prevail over what could arguably be referred to as the best army in the world. The man was a study in contradictions. He was short and slightly built with fine features and a pronounced profile that was at once striking and seemingly out of place on a soldier. His name was Moses Ezekiel and he was a Colonel in the Confederate Army.

This in and of itself was not remarkable except that Colonel Ezekiel was the first Jewish officer to rise to his current rank in the Confederate army. This was especially curious given the colonel's current assignment. He was the second-in-command of the newly formed Confederate Fenian Legion. This regiment was formed by taking men of Irish decent from the various units within the Confederate army and amalgamating them under the command of Major General Patrick Cleburne. Cleburne was a native Irishman who had gained some measure of fame during the War of the Rebellion and had the good sense to stay in the army and wait for someone to remember what he had done during the war.

That day was not long in coming for as soon as the trouble between the Confederacy and Great Britain was realized, a mobilization was undertaken. There was not an Irishman that had served in the war that did not have a reason to want revenge on the English. If for no other reason there was the systematic attempt at annihilation that the British had visited on the Irish people for the last two hundred years. Now with Cleburne in command and Ezekiel as his second in command, Cleburne felt that he had the force necessary to chase the minions of Queen Victoria back to where they came from or to send them to the nether regions where they belonged!

Not to be outdone, when word spread of the formation of the Fenian Legion, the U.S. Army General-in-Chief, Chamberlain, had authorized the re-constitution of the Old Irish Brigade. Chamberlain had seen first hand on the fields outside Fredericksburg at the foot of Marye's Heights just what kind of valor the Irish possessed. He would have liked to have their former commander, General Patrick Meagher take the reins again. This was not possible as Meagher was currently in Ireland trying to rally men to his most recent cause, chasing the English out of Canada. His efforts were of the highest intention but, he lacked the organizational skills and materiel to ensure success. His raid into Canada was doomed to fail. Only through sheer luck did Meagher escape with his life.

If Meagher was not available for the job, Grant wanted someone who had both the ethnic background as the men being commanded and who had also proven himself to be a capable leader under fire. When tasked to pick someone who could succeed Meagher to command the 'New Irish Brigade' as they were being called, for Chamberlain there was but one choice. The commander who had led troops of the Irish Brigade under fire at Marye's Heights and had not turned and run away. In that battle, this commander had to be ordered to withdraw. The man's name was St.Clair Mulholland, hero of the Irish Brigade's charge to the stone wall at Marye's Heights.

Mulholland was right on Ezekiel's heels and the two men fairly fought for the right to report to the assembled officers. Mulholland's rank won out in the end but he was gracious and kept his remarks brief stating simply, "Sirs, the Irish Brigade stands ready to attack on your orders and throw those smug English bastards back into the sea!"

Looks were exchanged among the command staff. Every man in the room knew of the centuries old hate between the Irish and the English but none had ever witnessed it first hand. Every man had the same thought, "And we have *two* regiments of men who feel the same as this man does? Almost makes you feel sorry for them. Almost."

Ezekiel waited until Mulholland had finished giving his report and, when he was acknowledged, came to attention, gave a crisp salute and made his report, which was almost a duplicate of the report given by the U.S. commander. The most notable exception was that the number of combat effectives for the Confederacy was less than those for the United States. Hood said, "No matter, what we lack in numbers we more than make up for in tenacity."

With all of the preparations made and all of the reports filed, everyone knew that all that was left to do was to wait. It was not in a soldier's manner to wait. Each man silently hoped to get this thing started. The sooner they got started, the sooner it would be over. It would be another two days before they got their wish.

CHAPTER 14

The Trap Is Laid

On the Outskirts of Richmond
December 21, 1870

For two days the two English regiments marched unmolested into the Virginia countryside. Their commanders grew more confident with every passing mile. Each thought, "At this rate, we'll be sitting in the capital rotunda by weeks end."

What the men could not have known was that there was never a moment where their movements were not observed and reported to the waiting bodies of armed men. Both Hood and Sherman silently hoped that their plan would work. Much would depend on the actions of the few selected men now waiting for the oncoming British troops.

If they broke and ran too soon, the trap would be revealed and any advantage would be lost. If they held too long, they ran the risk of being annihilated to a man. The two men selected to lead their respective elements were veterans of the last war and knew how to lead men into battle. The only thing that they could not count on was whether or not the British would fall for the elaborate ruse that had been prepared for them.

Sherman took Hood aside and said to him in a hushed voice, "Are you sure that the men can do this?"

Hood responded, "General, if any two groups of men can do this, they can. Our boys are all survivors of some of the toughest fighting from the last war as are yours. They know what is at stake and they will not let us down. It's just not in them to fail."

"I certainly hope you are right General Hood. If this plan fails then there is no force on Earth that can stop those people from coming here to Richmond and doing exactly what they set out to do." said Sherman as he scanned the horizon as if he could actually see what events were taking place some fifty miles distant.

"I agree that the plan has certain inherent risks but we must make the coming battle both swift and decisive. We must make it so costly for the British that they will desire nothing more than to leave this country. Neither your side nor ours can afford a prolonged conflict. We have both suffered great losses in the last war and it will take many years to heal the wounds and re-build what has been destroyed." Hood remarked.

Sherman nodded in agreement with Hood's observation. He knew all too well just what kind of precarious position the South was in. She had lost an entire generation of young men, her fields had been laid waste by traveling armies and that damage was only now beginning to heal itself. He had heard rumors that there hadn't been a decent crop of anything harvested in these parts for over five years. No, they could not afford a war of attrition, their victory would have to be swift and decisive as Hood observed.

Just as they were turning to leave the crest of the hill that they sat on, there came a deep rumble as if a storm were approaching. Both men turned toward the sound and then looked at each other and, without saying a word, both men conveyed the same thought to the other, "It's started". The rumble that they heard was not a storm as they both knew, but rather it was the deep booming of artillery. The plan had been for a small force to position itself in the mouth of a large valley shaped something like a shallow boat. Long and narrow, surrounded by high, rocky hills that still bore the signs of fighting that took place there nearly a decade ago. Among the mangled trees and rocks, the combined artillery of the United States and the Confederate States sat concealed until the Infantry did the job that it was assigned to do. Their job was to engage the enemy and make him advance.

They accomplished this by fighting what amounted to a rear guard action, meaning that their job was to delay the oncoming British forces and make them think that there was a larger force in front of them. This would make them eager to rush forward and finish off the main body of troops that they believed were ahead. In fact, there were no other troops in front of them save the five hundred or so that were firing and falling back by turns. To add to the confusion that was to be visited on the British, the men were dressed in civilian clothes to give the illusion that they were little more than home guard troops. This also had the effect of concealing the fact that they were soldiers from not one, but two armies. When they saw the group of men that had been firing on them sporadically, Fremantle and the other British officers were amused.

"They can't even send out an army to meet us", said Campbell.

Fremantle turned up his nose in his peculiar fashion and said, "If I had known that they were down to their militia, I should have advised Her Majesty to send the last graduating class from Sandhurst to fight these farmers!"

Norris, who was riding behind the two English officers, sensed that there was something more to what they were seeing. "I wouldn't get too comfortable Colonel Fremantle, something isn't right here. I have a very bad feeling about this."

Fremantle shot the former Confederate spy chief a withering glare and said, "Colonel Norris, perhaps you should stick to what you are good at which is spying and leave the real soldiering to those who have had the training to do so."

Norris shook his head and thought to himself, "Stubborn fool's going to get us all killed with that attitude."

It suddenly occurred to Norris that he needed to have

some sort of plan of escape if things went badly for his newfound friends. He had just about formed the details of that plan when it seemed that the whole world rose up around him with a brilliant flash and an ear-splitting roar. He had just enough time before he passed out to have the thought, "We've walked right into a trap and these idiots didn't even see it coming.

From his vantage point up among the rocks with the guns, Randall turned to the signalman behind him and said, "Send this message to General Lee. Your range is on target, fire for effect. Recommend a combination of percussion and timed fuse rounds."

The signalman wasted no time in making the necessary signals with his flags. Almost immediately came the reply, "Message received, will comply."

In the valley below, amidst the explosions, smoke and flying dirt and debris, Both Randall and Lee could see from their individual vantage points on opposite sides of the valley the destruction being visited upon the British troops. The majority of the soldiers had taken cover behind anything that they could find that offered any kind of protection. When it became apparent that they were not finding suitable targets for the guns, Randall signaled for them to cease firing. Now they would see if the next phase of the plan would work. As if by some unseen force, the remaining British troops rose up and reformed their ranks. Wounded and dead men could be seen scattered among the underbrush and rocks that made up the floor of the valley. Now, Randall could hear the faint sounds of orders being given and drums beating out the cadence of the march. "Just a few hundred yards more", he thought.

A casual observer might have accused both sides of scripting the battle; so predictable was the next chain of events. As the British troops began their next advance, they were taken under fire by the same group of men that had lured them into the valley. Again the small body of men fired and fell back. They gave up ground by the foot, leaving here and there some of their number who were unfortunate enough to present a target long enough for some British soldier to take aim and fire. When they had advanced about a half a mile into the valley, they saw that the way that they had come into the valley was not, in fact the only way in. Nor was the end that was being defended by the small group that opposed them the only way out.

When the officers and non-commissioned officers in the British force saw the ravine that branched off to the right side of the valley, they at once tried to seize upon it as an escape route. The orders were given to turn the main body of men into the ravine while leaving a small group of men to provide cover fire. Just as they were about to enter the ravine, which consisted of rolling terrain that would help conceal the retreating British troops, a shout was heard that sounded as if it were the crashing of waves upon the beach. Many of the British soldiers had served in Ireland prior to being posted to the elite units to which they now belonged and to a man they heard the all too familiar phrase "Faugh a Ballagh". This meant "Clear the way" it had become the battle cry of the Irish forces that were determined to chase the English out of their beloved land.

Now they could see where the yelling had come from. As they looked down the ravine, over a slight rise came the familiar green banner of the Irish Brigade of the United States army. However, the flag that flew at its side was one that they had not seen. It was a gaudy banner with a green canton and orange and white horizontal stripes. In the canton was the gold harp of Erin and the words "Fenian Legion" This was the new, predominately Irish unit that had been formed for just this purpose. It was at that moment that to a man, they felt real fear. Most of them knew of the intense hatred that the Irish had for the English. What they did not realize is that when many of them immigrated to this New World, they brought that hate with them. They would soon discover just how deep that hate ran.

As the British troops began to maneuver from column of fours into the familiar two ranks of 'line of battle' their officers directed them via the sergeants and corporals to get them into a formation that would maximize their firepower and at the same time, minimize the risk of their flanks being turned or their lines being broken. Just as they were finishing the last few movements that would produce a nearly solid wall of men and muskets, the 'Irish' troops did something that totally mystified and confused the British troops and their commanders as well, they suddenly and without any command or signal, broke formation and began seeking shelter amongst the trees and rocks and, firing from these concealed and entrenched positions began to have a telling effect on the solid mass of red-coated British troops not more than one hundred yards distant.

As the battle seemingly began to fall apart, Fremantle and Campbell began to look about them for some way to regroup their men and to bring them out of this ambush. Men were falling all around them some one at a time, some in groups of two or three. Just when the British commanders began to think things could not get worse, they did. Now that the Confederate infantry was under cover and not out on the open field like the British troops were, the artillery began again with devastating results. Randall and Lee began to rain down round after deadly round of exploding shot, spherical case shot and, for those guns positioned close enough to make effective use of it, canister shot.

This last particular piece of ordnance was savagely effective. At ranges of six hundred yards or less, cannon which normally fired a solid or exploding projectile ranging in size from three to roughly four and a half inches, now took to firing what amounted to large tin cans packed tightly with a payload of anywhere from fifty to seventy-five lead or wrought iron balls, some almost an inch in diameter. When loaded into an artillery piece with an eight to ten ounce charge of black gunpowder and with zero degrees of elevation, you now effectively have the equivalent of a large bore shotgun capable of cutting huge gaps in an enemy's lines. If things got really desperate, you would simply load two of these deadly canister rounds into the barrel, essentially doubling the already horrific effectiveness of the round.

Many of the men either manning the cannons or now occupying the covered ground at the base of the hills surrounding the valley had seen first hand what this type of artillery work was capable of. Such as those men who had seen a full company of their fellows march into Cushing's battery at Gettysburg and simply cease to exist, this was something that the British troops had not experienced and were not prepared for. As their ranks were being raked by rifle fire and then, suddenly artillery fire started blasting huge, gaping holes in their ranks, many of the British soldiers had simply had enough and many began to turn and run away. Many could not because they were either pinned down by what they now realized was definitely more than simple militia but was, in fact trained infantry or they were too busy trying to stay out of the way of the multitude of canister shot that seemed to be buzzing around their heads like so many angry hornets.

For the men who were trapped, they would soon learn that this may actually be a blessing in disguise. Just as the first small group of men was reaching the entrance to this small 'Valley of the Shadow of Death' as some would later call it, they heard a new sound that suddenly sounded like the death rattle of a man dying a slow, painful death. It occurred to them quickly, but unfortunately not quickly enough, just what they were hearing...cavalry!

CHAPTER 15
BOOTS AND SADDLES

Thinking themselves in the clear and heading back to the ships that brought them to their current misfortune, the first group of men heard what they mistook for the rumble of thunder and the welcome relief and covering shroud of lowered visibility that the accompanying rain would bring. They knew that if it started to rain and the rains came hard and fast enough, the men that had ambushed them in that small valley would most likely not pursue them. What they would discover was that instead of relief this particular brand of 'thunder' only brought with it the promise of more pain and suffering for these poor unfortunate sons of England who now realized that they were very, very far from home and were not likely to ever get back there again.

The first of the horsemen rounded the rocks and trees that lined the entrance to the valley and was met with a sight that he would relate to his grandchildren almost fifty years later. He saw before him an open field and in the middle of that field were literally hundreds of scurrying men, all running and, few if any, stopping to load and fire their muskets.

As he watched from a vantage point a the rear of the oncoming column, General Devin remarked to the man beside him, "Well, General Stuart, it appears that the infantry and artillery have saved some work for us to do."

"It does indeed, sir", replied Stuart in his characteristic, boyish, enthusiasm. Stuart then took out a small pad of paper and the stub of a pencil from an inside jacket pocket, scribbled a note and, calling for a courier, handed him the note with the following instructions,

"Take this message to Generals Randall, Lee, Sherman and Hood, with my compliments on a job well done. Advise Generals Randall and Lee that we are about to enter the field and that they may cease their artillery barrage so that our cavalry will not be at risk. Advise Generals Sherman and Hood that they may continue to press the enemy at whatever advantage they may see fit. We will attack those people as we previously have arranged but we will also be ready to lend support to the infantry if needed. Request Generals Hood and Sherman to advise all company commanders, battalion commanders and brigade commanders of our intentions and advise them to take the necessary steps needed to allow them the flexibility to quickly react to any possible breakthroughs that the cavalry my cause".

With those words the courier left in search of the various commanders as ordered. Stuart turned to General Devin and said, "General Devin, would you please order the charge, sir?"

"It would be my great pleasure General Stuart." Devin replied. With those words, he turned to his bugler and said, "Sergeant, sound the advance."

The bugler blew the tune that would signal the beginning of the end for the British troops trapped in the valley. The attack was brilliant in its simplicity. The combined cavalry force would attack en echelon. Their staggered formation was nearly indefensible and would permit almost no chance for the infantry to escape. Those who were not killed would be forced to surrender. Those who would not surrender would be shown no mercy.

Arms at the ready, the troopers moved forward at a gallop. As they closed the distance with the infantry, it was clear to see that nearly all of the fight was gone from all but the most stalwart soldiers in the British ranks. Those who stood were soon cut down and those who ran had the misfortune of being driven into the waiting ranks of infantry. It took only an hour and forty minutes until the British commanders showed the white flag and rode out to discuss terms of surrender with their enemy.

The ground between the two groups of men was littered with the bodies of the dead and wounded from both sides. All around them they heard the cries of the wounded. Fremantle and Campbell rode forward to parley with the representatives of the army that had so soundly beaten them. On the other end of the field, it was decided that as a show of solidarity between the two former enemies, one officer from the Confederate army and one from the U.S.

Army would ride forward and deliver the terms under which the defeated British troops would lay down their arms. The officers selected for this duty were two who had learned warfare under some of the worst conditions imaginable. From the streets of Mexico City to the fields around Fredericksburg, the two men had seen and experienced the horrors of war that only other soldiers can begin to understand.

Fremantle saw the two men riding out under their own white flag and when they were within a hundred yards he muttered to Campbell, "Oh dear God, they've sent Jackson!"

Campbell's eyes grew wide and his head snapped around to face Fremantle and with a look of abject horror he said, "That's not the worst of it, look who is with him!"

Both men turned to look at the figure beside Jackson in the dusty blue uniform of the U.S. Army. Tall and rugged looking with just a hint of gray in his short cropped red hair, William Tecumseh Sherman wore on his face the same chiseled scowl that had become his trademark throughout his years in the Western theater of the War Between the States.

His eyes constantly moved about, scanning the surrounding countryside for any sign of treachery. He whispered to Jackson, "Are you sure that our boys know what to do if this goes badly General?"

Jackson, with his trademark cadet cap pulled low as to almost cover his eyes, stared straight ahead and replied,

"General, if anything untoward happens to us, there won't be a man left alive to get back to their boats, If we hadn't already sunk 'em!"

Jackson was referring to the mission carried out by the same group of men that had initially observed the British landing. Their orders were to quietly approach the boats, overpower and take prisoner the men guarding them and send them to the bottom of the Chesapeake. Using their now trademark technique of muffling their horses and equipment, the men were able to move within a few hundred yards of the British sentries and then, on foot, moving in to subdue them. Everything went nearly perfect except that a sentry observed one of the men's movements.

The British soldier nearly sounded the alarm. But only nearly, a second man who was an expert with nearly any kind of weapon imaginable was able to kill the sentry at a distance of nearly thirty feet with a large knife thrown as true as any bullet or arrow ever fired. With the job done and only one man killed on either side, the men considered themselves extremely fortunate. Now they had only to wait for further word of the battle and any orders that may arise from that arena.

Meanwhile back on the field, Fremantle, Campbell, Jackson and Sherman were sitting cross-legged, Indian style on the ground discussing the situation at hand. Fremantle was not at all happy about being bested by what he considered to be a "rag-tag band of rebels being abetted by the army of a foreign government who had no right to interfere with Great Britain and her legitimate interests on the North American continent."

Campbell was a bit more circumspect. His only comment to Fremantle before they sat down to talk was, "I beg you General, do be careful what you say to these two I daresay from their reputations during the late war, I doubt that you can expect much in the way of quarter from them!"

Fremantle snorted in disdain and said, "Oh stuff and nonsense Campbell, they are obliged to release us as we both hold diplomatic status in the Queen's government. Oh, they may fuss and bluster but they wouldn't dare do anything remotely threatening to us."

For his own part, Campbell was not too sure and was not about to take any chances. He said, "All the same old boy, I suggest we hear them out before we try taking the hard line with them."

Fremantle shook his head and thought to himself, "Passable officer, no future as a diplomat though."

As the drama on the field unfolded before them, nearly every man on either side of the field had his attention on the four men now deciding their fates. Except one. Ever since the battle had turned against the British, Norris had been searching for a way out. He was sure he found it when he saw an old dry creek bed that disappeared through some dense underbrush that created what amounted to as not much more than a game trail moving away from the fighting.

He quickly looked around to see if anyone was watching him and when it was clear that everyone was otherwise engaged, He slipped away down the shallow depression that had been the creek bed and bending low, he made his way out of this valley of death that had almost claimed him. With his ears still ringing from the near miss of the artillery shell, he moved as quickly and as quietly as he could in the direction that he thought would lead him back to the boats. Once there he would order one of them to take him back to the fleet where he would report that Fremantle, Campbell and all their men were lost.

Norris was lost in this latest bit of revelry when he thought that he heard something moving in the brush nearby. He stopped and found a large bush to hide behind. After several minutes went by he stood up and began heading in the direction of the bay. He hadn't gone very far when he entered a pine thicket and thought he caught a flash of movement to his left. He had just about made up his mind that it had been an animal that he had startled, when he started out again and suddenly heard the distinctive sound of metal on metal. Knowing full well that the sound could only have been produced by a human and also knowing that he was unlikely to encounter anyone out here that was not part of the deadly game that was now playing out in the valley only a half mile or so distant, Norris froze. He spotted a likely hiding spot where a large pine tree had been shattered by what appeared to have been lightning but could have also been from a shell fired in the last war. He moved around behind the fallen bole of the tree, using the nearly three foot thick trunk and its numerous branches to break up the outline of his shape.

It nearly worked; the man following Norris had almost walked past him. Not that Norris posed any great threat to the man. Norris had neglected to arm himself prior to fleeing the battle. What's more, he had foolishly retained his bright red coat, the one that he was so proud to have been allowed to wear for the past five and a half years. Seeing a flash of the former spy leader's coat, Sergeant Major Lester Addison of the newly reconstituted Stonewall Brigade turned. He trained his rifle on the spot on the man's chest where the two buff leather belts crossed. This spot was roughly where the man's heart would be and both men knew it. Slowly Norris rose from his hiding place and said, "Fairly done Sergeant Major, I am your prisoner."

Norris slowly reached down and drew his sword from its scabbard. The sword was a showpiece, not of the type made for combat. Norris turned the hilt toward Addison and offered it in a sign of surrender.

Addison took the proffered weapon and, never taking his eyes off of Norris ordered him to sit down at the base of a large tree. Norris was momentarily confused, he believed that he would be hurried back to the battlefield and presented to the enemy leaders as some sort of prize. Suddenly, he looked at the man's face and there before him in a memory stood another man from another time and this time it was Norris who had the advantage of a weapon. The time was several years previous when Norris was assisting the British government in ferreting out all of the Confederate agents who were sending back information to Lee and Longstreet.

The man was clearly frightened, as if he had seen a ghost. Indeed that was exactly what his first thought was. He had come to believe as many of his fellow agents had, that Norris had died during his attempted escape from the Confederate capital shortly after his part in the attempted coup had been discovered. Now, Norris stood before him holding a large revolver and saying, "Look David, its really quite simple, either you go to work for me or you go for a long swim in the Thames. At this the younger man grew indignant. He scowled at the former Confederate spy chief and said, "No *Major*, I'm not a traitor like you! Kill me if you want, I will not turn my back on my duty to my country like you did!"

This enraged Norris and without another thought, he raised the pistol and shot the man twice in the chest. At a distance of less than six feet, the impact of the bullets lifted the man off of his feet and threw him nearly ten feet backward where he landed in a heap, dead before he hit the ground. Norris looked at the body of the former Confederate operative lying in the street and thought, "What is this world coming to, a spy who is an idealist?" With that thought, he turned and made his way back to

Buckingham Palace to report on this latest failure to gain an advantage against the Confederate government. Now it was Addison's turn for a moment of reverie. He thought about the last time he had seen the young man some ten years his junior. They were sitting at the kitchen table in Addison's home in Richmond and he was saying to the other man, "David, I don't like this, it doesn't feel right. England's a long way from Richmond, who will you go to if you need help? Who's going to look out for you?"

The younger man frowned and said, "Lester, I'm nearly twenty eight years old, I can look after myself. Besides I don't remember Mama and Papa bestowing the mantle of responsibility for my well being squarely on your shoulders."

"Easy little brother, I just don't want anything to happen to you. Now that Mama and Papa are gone, you're the only family that I have left and I don't want to lose you unnecessarily."

The younger man looked down at the tabletop not wanting to meet his older brother's gaze. Both men had served in the War, Lester in the 33rd Virginia and David in the Confederate Secret Service. It was his younger brother's decision to go into the shadowy world of espionage that had always bewildered the elder Addison. In his mind, the only way to defeat an enemy was to face him across that still small space and crush him with superior numbers or outmaneuver him on the field. He never once thought about attacking an enemy from behind the lines or better yet from within his own ranks. The more he thought about it, the more he saw that the risks his brother took were often times greater than his own. At least when he faced an enemy on the field of battle, either he killed his enemy or his enemy would kill him.

He had been fortunate enough to escape many engagements with his life. He was wounded slightly at First Manassas but had managed to capture an enemy flag, which won him a promotion to Corporal. From there other deeds and other engagements had shown his superiors that here was a man who could be depended on to get the job done. He was promoted through the ranks until he attained the rank of First Sergeant. It was this rank that he held at the end of the War.

Now that they had won their independence, he was at a loss as to where to go next. The family farm had been razed and it would be years before the damage was repaired. It was then that he saw an advertisement in the Richmond paper stating that they were looking for former soldiers to act as security guards inside the Executive mansion. They wanted men with combat experience who knew how to read men's faces and the way that their bodies moved when they were up to something. They wanted men who knew how to fight and defend themselves and others. In short, they wanted Lester Addison, former First Sergeant in the 33rd Virginia Infantry Regiment.

He made his application that same day and within a matter of two days, a telegram came for him stating that he was being hired for the position and that the pay would be the handsome sum of twenty dollars a month. It was nearly twice what he earned as a soldier and it would be enough to sustain him and at the same time he could get the farm back to its former productive self. Addison was less enthusiastic about his brother's post-War fortunes. David had opted to remain in the Secret Service. He jumped at the opportunity to earn *thirty* dollars a month *and* he would get the chance to travel and see distant lands that most men his age only dreamed about.

Despite his objections and the hours spent cajoling and haranguing his brother about the folly of his decision, Lester was there at the docks to see his brother off on this great adventure that he was undertaking. He never mentioned it to David but, as the two men said their goodbyes, Lester had the overwhelming sense that he would never see his younger brother again. It would take three years for this prophecy to be fulfilled but it would come to pass.

Now Norris saw something else in the man's eyes. It wasn't compassion or the hard bitter look of a man who was about to do his duty, this was something that Norris had never seen before but for all that he knew just what it was, the look of a man out for revenge. He looked at the man and said, "Sergeant Major, I don't suppose that you would entertain the possibility that we might make some sort of financial arrangement would you?

Addison's cold stare and his silence said more than

words ever could. There would be no deals, no chance of escape. Now Norris felt afraid, he sputtered, "Look here, I don't know what you're thinking but believe me, I am much more valuable to you alive than dead."

Still Addison said nothing. Norris tried again. "I demand that you take me to your superiors as I am guaranteed protection as a prisoner under the rules of war!"

Still there was no indication that Addison was even listening. Finally, in a last desperate effort to save himself, Norris said, "I have information that your government would find useful, information about an attempt to subvert the government itself. I can give you names, dates, anything you want. Think about it, with this information, you could win yourself a commission!"

Addison's features softened a moment then went back to their former chiseled appearance. He looked at the traitor Norris and said, "You mean information about the coup attempt on President Davis? We found out about that not six months after the plan was implemented. As for names, we don't need them. We rounded up everyone involved and now they're either dead or sitting in Libby prison wishing that they were. I say we rounded up everyone, everyone that is except you and Colonel, I mean *General* Fremantle. But after this, I don't think that's a problem anymore."

At these words, Norris' face lost all its color and he began to back pedal away from Addison as if the man were evil incarnate. But before he could gain his feet and run, Addison hauled him up by his jacket lapel, having set his rifle down during the previous exchange but still holding the sword in one hand, loose and not threatening. He backed the man against a large tree, stepped in close until their noses almost touched. It was at this point Addison smiled an evil grin at Norris and said, "You want to discuss names? Well, here's a name for you. You should recognize this name, since you killed the man it belonged to! How about the name David Addison? Does that bring anyone to mind for you? Well it does for me, you see, David Addison was my younger brother and you murdered him you filthy bastard!"

Norris tried to break free of the man's grip but it was not to be. As Lester Addison was venting his fury upon Norris, he was carefully backing the man up against a tree and, once he had him there, he took Norris' own sword and, summoning up every ounce of strength, every drop of emotion and all the fury that his heart contained, he raised the sword and plunged it into the man's chest at the same point that his rifle had been trained on just moments before.

The look on Norris's face changed from one of fear to one of a mixture of surprise and extreme agony. The blade of the sword, just over three feet long, traversed the man's chest cavity, damaging organs, severing arteries until it reached the ribs connected to Norris' spinal column. There the point of the blade passed between two ribs, severing the cartilage between them and, now free of the man's body, embedded itself in the tree behind him. Norris now hung, suspended like an insect in some obscene bug collection. The last thing his eyes saw were the face of David Addison's older brother just a few inches from his own. The last sound his ears heard were the voice of Lester Addison saying, "See you in Hell, traitor."

With that Norris died. His body was found days later after the battle was over and the search for survivors and the dead was begun. No one knew how Norris came to be where he was found and no one knew who had done the deed. If anyone knew, they weren't talking. The only things that were known for certain were, Norris was killed for revenge. This was obvious from the note left by the body. It read, 'Ever thus shall be the fate of traitors.' The other certainty was that the Confederacy would not be losing any more agents in its Secret Service.

Now would begin the long task of cleaning up and repairing the country as best they could. Now began the task of getting back to the business of living. No one was more keenly aware of this than the man who had to see that it got done, President James Longstreet. It was this Herculean task that now sat squarely on his shoulders. He wondered just how the job would get done and moreover, he wondered how he was going to deal with the British. Letters arrived almost daily demanding the release of General Fremantle. The rest of the British troops, at least those healthy enough to travel had been taken to their boats and sent back to England.

Since he had merely been a soldier following the orders of a superior, General Campbell was released with his men. Once they signed parole papers stating that they admitted that their actions were of a criminal nature and that they agreed to never take up arms against the Confederacy *or* the United States of America ever again, they were given back their arms and their colors (much to the dismay of the two Irish Regiments that had been instrumental in their defeat). And marched the entire distance from Richmond to the spot on the Chesapeake Bay where their transports were waiting.

The march had been long and bitterly cold, owing to the fact that it was now nearing the end of December. Add to that the fact that they were prodded (literally) at every step by the bayonets of the Irishmen who seemed to take some small consolation at not being able to keep the British Regimental flags by being allowed to torment their owners the entire trip back to the boats. Once there, the soldiers were herded on board the boats and then they were escorted by several ships of the line out of Confederate territorial waters and, beyond that by a pair of U.S. Navy frigates among them the *Harriet Lane*, commanded by Rear Admiral O'Kane.

Still not wanting to appear any less the sailor, O'Kane was aloft in the rigging as the transports drew alongside. He came down carefully and once on the deck, he went to the portside rail and hailed the closest transport. When the reply came back from Admiral Sir James Allerton who they were, O'Kane's eyebrows shot up and he let out a soft whistle, remarking to the man holding the megaphone, "Boy, when they send one of their ships, they don't just send it out with any old Jack Tar, they send their best!"

O'Kane sent his regards to the Admiral and said that the *Harriet Lane* would accompany *Repulse* out as far as the twelve mile limit where she would turn back and the British ship could continue on to Portsmouth or whatever port she saw fit to make for. With his duty done, O'Kane gave the helmsman the course that would take them back home and he would then report to the Navy Department for his next posting. He was already thinking about who should command the *Harriet Lane* after his departure. Her second-in-command was an able commander and a good all around seaman. He would give her good service till the end of her days in the fleet. O'Kane figured she had about ten more good years left in her barring any serious damage or stresses.

"Yes, just enough time for the man to make his flag. It will be a fitting and proper end to two long, eventful careers. It's no less than they deserve after all that they've been through." O'Kane thought and then smiled.

CHAPTER 16
SECOND CHANCES
RICHMOND
SPRING 1871

Longstreet sat on the veranda attached to the rear of the Executive Mansion, enjoying the breeze and watching the humming birds flitting around the arbor that was covered in wisteria and honeysuckle. "Oh to be as carefree as they are," he thought. Still, Longstreet couldn't complain too loudly. He had just come back from a very low-key but highly important meeting with President Grant to discuss the repercussions of the battle that had been fought just a couple of months before.

"I don't know if I would do what you are suggesting Pete", Grant had said.

"I know it sounds risky Sam, but the man has caused too much suffering and death to just walk away scot-free." Longstreet countered.

"I agree but the Queen has been making inquiries about our assisting them with gaining his release. I don't know how much longer I can put her off. Pretty soon she'll have justification for sending troops." Grant shook his head as he related this last bit of information to his counterpart.

Longstreet considered what Grant had said and then announced that he had made a decision in the matter. "Alright Sam, here's what we'll do. You'll tell Her Majesty that we are holding General Fremantle for questioning on a possible criminal matter to which he may or may not have prior knowledge. That should keep her happy until we sort this thing out."

Grant sighed and said, "Okay Pete, I'll try it and see if she will go for it. In the meantime, you need to figure out what you think the appropriate punishment is."

"I know what the appropriate punishment is Sam, I just don't know if we could get away with it." At this both men chuckled grimly at Longstreet's attempt at dark humor.

What was needed here, both men agreed was an object lesson that neither the man nor his country would ever forget. Suddenly, as if some invisible telegraph wire that communicated their thoughts to one another somehow connected them, the two men said in unison, "I just had an idea."

They looked at one another for a moment then Grant said, "Are you thinking the same thing that I am?"

Longstreet replied, "I think so and if it works, we could well be rid of the English for a long time to come." Then the two men began to exchange ideas on how best to deal with the man who had very nearly destroyed not one but two countries from within.

At 2 o'clock the next morning, Fremantle, dressed in the drab woolen garb of a prisoner was roused from a sound sleep in his cell in the county jail where he had been quartered ever since his arrest on the field that fateful day. Dazed and in a state of utter confusion, Fremantle was shackled and led from the cell by six very large, surly men with wooden truncheons who's purpose left very little to the imagination. They led Fremantle out and placed him in the back of a buckboard and started off down the street at a slow pace. "At least I'm not sitting on a coffin" thought Fremantle, referring to the custom of the day where a condemned man was made to ride to his execution on the top of the coffin which would soon be used to bury him.

Had he but known his destination, Fremantle may well have wished for that coffin. The buckboard made several twists and turns in its trek to get where it was going due not in any small part to the remaining debris that had not yet been cleared away from the massive devastation wrought during the War of the Rebellion.

When they passed through what appeared to be the remains of the city's central plaza, Fremantle began to recognize several of the buildings were amazingly intact and there still street signs every now and then. Fremantle thought that they might actually be taking him to the docks to catch a boat back to England. As if reading his thoughts, the man riding next to the driver turned and, with a malevolent grin on his face said,

"Don't worry General, we're taking you back to the boats so that you can go home to England and tell your precious Queen Victoria just how badly you had been treated by the enemies of the Crown. We've got to take you to get cleaned up and changed into something more presentable. But first, we have a little side trip to make. It won't take long, besides, there are some old friends of yours that I happen to have it on good authority are very anxious to see you again."

It was just about sunrise when they began to slow down the buckboard as they approached their destination. Fremantle turned to see what the driver and his passenger where looking at when he saw the large brick building and the sign that announced to all who saw it that, like the sign over the gates of Hell in Dante's Divine Comedy or Inferno as it is better known, all hope was to be abandoned once one entered into, Libby Prison. Fremantle's eyes grew wide with fear when he realized what the two men had planned for him. Images of torture and of a painful death filled his imagination as the buckboard turned to make its way up the gravel path to the infamous prison where once Federal officers had been held until exchanged. It was also the sight of one of the most daring escape attempts known in the modern age. Of 109 officers that began the escape, most were re-captured and returned to captivity. Only a small number of men actually made good their escape and returned to Union lines.

The buckboard came to a stop outside a heavy wooden door bound with iron straps and hung on huge iron hinges that would make breaking the door down a near impossibility. One of the men went to the door and knocked on it, using the large iron ring hung there for that very purpose. After a moment or two, the sound of a large bolt being drawn back could be heard from inside the prison. A moment later a guard appeared and escorted the three men inside. Once inside, Fremantle was shocked to see the squalid conditions that existed. In the dimly lit interior he could swear he could see rats running back and forth on the floor, oblivious to the passing of the group. Insects of the basest variety scurried up the walls and across the floors as they passed.

By now Fremantle's senses were becoming overloaded with the sights, smells, and sounds of this most dreadful of places. From time to time they would pass a large wooden door of the same variety through which they entered the building but in some cases they would hear low moans from behind the doors and on one occasion, through a hole at the bottom of the door used to pass food buckets and night jars, a hand reached out for them. The sight of that hand, almost skeletal in its gaunt paleness, shook Fremantle to the very core of his being and he almost tried to run. Sensing this the guard simply said, "I wouldn't try it. You wouldn't make the outer fence before the guards on the roof shot you dead."

Now the gravity of his situation began to take hold. He was almost in tears and had begun to talk to himself in wildly ranting tirades when the group stopped outside another such door. This one lacked any of the sights and sounds of the previous ones. Instead, all was deathly still and quiet. Not knowing now what lie in store for him, Fremantle hung back waiting. The guard took out a large ring with several keys on it and began trying them in the keyhole. After only a minute or two, he found the right one and turned it in the large brass lock. When the shank of the lock opened, the guard removed it from the hasp and pulled the door open.

The first thing that Fremantle experienced was the overpowering stench of the room. It was a mixture of sweat, smoke, spoiled food and human waste. He fought, albeit briefly the urge to vomit but the smell was too intense to resist. Once he regained his composure, the guard took him by the arm and propelled him toward the interior of the cell. There was a small amount of light from a few candle stubs so Fremantle could see very little in the room. As he crossed the threshold and entered the room, the guard slammed the door shut and Fremantle heard the lock being replaced in the hasp and being locked.

Trying to adjust his eyes to the available light, Fremantle began to take stock of his surroundings. He noted high, smooth walls with small windows near the top and almost nothing in the way of furnishings save for a small table and a couple of wooden chairs. The floor was strewn with dirty straw and on one occasion, Fremantle could have sworn he heard or saw a rat move across the room. As the light increased over the next few hours, Fremantle, now sitting at the small table, was able to detect something else in the room that he had missed before. Gathered in a tight group in one corner of the room were the shapes of a dozen or so sleeping men. They were huddled together, some covered with thin, threadbare blankets all trying to stave off the cool night air.

As the sun began to shine down through the windows, the men began to stir. Fremantle had managed to doze off briefly once or twice during the night. Slowly in ones and twos, the men began to sit up and, trying not to disturb the men around them got up and made their way to the bucket in the corner that served as their latrine. Most moved around the cell in a wooden, mechanical manner. Presently though, one fellow turned in his direction and, calling out to his cellmates said, "Well what do you know boys, looks like one of the guards slipped us a fresh fish."

Several of the others chuckled derisively but one man looked in Fremantle's direction and said, "I know you, you're the one that got me involved in that whole uprising mess that got me sent here!"

Soon others were looking at him and one even managed to recall his name saying, "Sure, I know him. He's that bastard Englishman, Fremantle. If I had the strength enough to do it, I'd wring his rotten neck."

With that, the men all stood and as one mass, made their way across the cell in Fremantle's direction. Soon they were upon him and they pummeled and beat him to the point where he thought they would kill him. Just then, from their observation point outside the cell, the guard and the two men who brought him to this accursed place, entered the cell, pulled the prisoners off him and hauled him to his feet. Beaten, bruised and bloody with one eye blackened and almost swollen shut, he was taken from the cell and returned to the county jail where he had previously been held.

A doctor was called in to examine him he was cleaned up and after a short, cursory examination, pronounced alive and sound. Yes he was alive, however sound was another matter altogether. The tally of his injuries included the aforementioned black eye, a broken nose, three cracked ribs and a host of bruises, abrasions and small cuts.

As bad as the man looked, he felt infinitely worse. Not only was he suffering from his physical condition, the entire experience had left an indelible mark on the man's psyche. It was these invisible scars that he would return with to England and become a staunch opponent to any further attempts to re-take the American colonies lost nearly a century before. He was even said to have been critical of the Queen's handling of the whole War Between the States and the military action taken in 1870-1871. He quietly slipped into obscurity and was rarely seen outside the grounds of his estate after 1873. Thus ended the most critical set of events to face the fledgling republic since she won her independence nearly a decade before. Now she was faced with the almost insurmountable task of rebuilding and restoring the nation to its former state. It was this task that Longstreet was musing about on the veranda on this fine spring day. As if by some strange cosmic design, a courier rode up to the gate near where Longstreet sat. He dismounted and entered the yard speaking briefly to the guard posted at the gate. He approached Longstreet on the heels of the guard and after a brief exchange between the guard and Longstreet, the courier was allowed to approach the President. He made his apologies for disturbing the President and without fanfare handed him a letter. Longstreet looked at the envelope and tried to determine its origins. He could see that it was written in a strong hand and he thought that he could almost identify the sender. No return address was listed but the quality of the paper gave some indication that the letter did not come from some angry farmer complaining about unexploded ordnance from the last war going off and killing a couple of his best cows. He opened the letter and there at the top center of the page was the Great Seal of the United States. He now realized whose hand had written the letter, his old friend, Sam Grant, President of the United States. The letter was an invitation for Longstreet to visit Grant in Washington City at the White House. Longstreet went to his desk and took out a sheet of stationary with the Great Seal of the Confederacy located in just the same place as the seal on Grant's letter. He quickly penned a response in the affirmative and then, sealing it in an envelope, handed it to the courier with the instructions that this should see none but President Grant's own hand. The courier nodded his understanding, turned and left the grounds. Now he would see what type of neighbor the United States intended to be. He could not have imagined what would soon take place.

EPILOGUE

April, 1871
Washington, D.C.

The two old friends sat side by side on the settee in the Oval Office. Grant turned to Longstreet and said, "Thanks for coming Pete, I wanted to have the opportunity to talk to you myself, alone to find out how things were going and where you stand with the rebuilding process."

"Well", said Longstreet, "we have our good days and bad days as you well know, but we are making progress. We have most of the roads back up to standard and the railroads are coming along. The one thing that we are having a problem with is finding enough good quality seed and fertilizer to re-vitalize our farms. We can't go to England to get them because of the last bit of unpleasantness and France is in worse shape than we are because of Bonaparte. I don't know what else to do."

Grant looked at his friend, genuinely concerned and said, "Well Pete, you haven't asked us yet!"

Longstreet's face took on a look of astonishment. "I never thought that you would even consider letting us approach any businesses here."

"Why not? You yourself said once that what we needed was a gate in the fence between our two countries." replied Grant.

Longstreet laughed and said, "This is just like our days at the Point, you always using my own words against me."

Both men laughed and spoke of other official business, Grant wanting to know about the state of the Confederacy's internal struggles, and the Government in general. Longstreet gave Grant all of the details, Pickett was warming to the post of Vice President, the various officers were working hard to rebuild their commands. The Navy had been refitting some of its ships and was in the market to add one or two new ships to their fleet. Grant made a mental note to speak to Dahlgren about the possibility of selling a couple of the U.S. Navy's older ships to the Confederacy to help shore up their fleet. Then Longstreet gave Grant some news that he hadn't expected.

On a more personal note, General and Mrs. Jackson had become parents again, this time to a healthy baby boy. Grant was delighted. "Those two need about six more!" he laughed. His demeanor changed to a more solemn tone when Longstreet informed him of the name that they had selected for the boy. "Robert Lee Jackson. Old Jack fairly worshipped the man you know, we all did." Longstreet said wistfully.

Grant nodded and said, "A man is never truly dead until he is forgotten. Let's all hope we never forget men of his kind."

Longstreet nodded in agreement.

Then Grant shocked his old friend by asking, "So tell me Pete, honestly, will she hold together?"

"Who?" said Longstreet.

"The Confederacy," said Grant.

Longstreet's eyes dropped to a spot on the floor between his feet and slowly replied, "I don't know Sam, we're trying everything we know to keep her afloat and some things work, others don't. The way I see it if we can make it through the next two years, we have a fair chance. If anything else happens like we just went through, we're doomed."

Grant sighed, put his hand on his friends arm and said, "I wish you all the best Pete; I really do. Just remember that if it all starts to fall apart, we will always welcome you back."

At this, Longstreet's head snapped up and he looked Grant squarely in the eye and said, "Do you think that the people would? Old wounds run deep and aren't easily forgotten. It might not be so easy."

Grant smiled and shook his head, "Nothing worth having ever is, is it? We'll just have to wait and see what happens next."